S0-AFO-041

the coast road

PETER CORRIS is known as the 'Godfather' of Australian crime fiction through his Cliff Hardy detective stories. He has written in many other areas, including a co-authored autobiography of the late Professor Fred Hollows, a history of boxing in Australia, spy novels, historical novels and a collection of short stories revolving around the game of golf. He is married to writer Jean Bedford and lives on the Illawarra coast, south of Sydney. They have three daughters.

PETER CORRIS

the coast road

A CLIFF HARDY NOVEL

ALLEN&UNWIN

All characters and events in this book are fictitious. There is no police station in Bellambi.

First published in 2004

Copyright © Peter Corris 2004

All rights reserved. No part of this book may be reproduced or transmitted in any form or by any means, electronic or mechanical, including photocopying, recording or by any information storage and retrieval system, without prior permission in writing from the publisher. The *Australian Copyright Act 1968* (the Act) allows a maximum of one chapter or 10 per cent of this book, whichever is the greater, to be photocopied by any educational institution for its educational purposes provided that the educational institution (or body that administers it) has given a remuneration notice to Copyright Agency Limited (CAL) under the Act.

Allen & Unwin
83 Alexander Street
Crows Nest NSW 2065
Australia
Phone: (61 2) 8425 0100
Fax: (61 2) 9906 2218
Email: info@allenandunwin.com
Web: www.allenandunwin.com

National Library of Australia
Cataloguing-in-Publication entry:

Corris, Peter, 1942– .
   The coast road.

   ISBN 1 74114 384 5.

   1. Hardy, Cliff (Fictitious character) – Fiction.
   2. Private investigators – Fiction. I. Title. (Series:
   Cliff Hardy; no. 26).

A823.3

Set in 12/14 pt Adobe Garamond by Midland Typesetters
Printed in Australia by McPherson's Printing Group

10 9 8 7 6 5 4 3

For Heather Wearne and Kate Ravenswood

Acknowledgments

For help in the writing phase, thanks to Jean Bedford and my friends in the Illawarra. For editorial expertise, thanks again to Jean and to Jo Jarrah.

1

It had to happen sooner or later. The building in St Peters Lane where I've had my office for longer than I like to think about has come up for 'restoration'. Read demolition maybe, with a retained façade. I knew the hammer was poised when my lease ran out and all I was offered was a fortnightly tenancy. I took it and hung on as long as I could, but the game's up. The rent's been cheap because of the condition of the joint. DDD, my ex and now late wife Cyn called it—dark, damp and dusty. And that was years ago. It's had a few facelifts, paint jobs, rewiring, but the space had just become too potentially valuable to accommodate tenants like me.

We held a party—Stephanie Geller, astrologer, Frank Corso, antiquarian bookseller, Lucille Harvey, genealogist, Donald Carver, philatelist, Henri Baden, numismatist and a few others, some of whom imported and exported, and me. Strictly cheap wine casks, paper cups, Salada biscuits, cheese slices.

'Usually they offer the existing tenants first option on the new offices,' Don Carver said. Don looks like a bird, with a long nose and retreating chin. He's slumped as if all those years of peering through magnifying glasses have bent him over.

Frank Corso held a three-tier Salada and cheese slice construction in one hand and a brimful cup of rough red in the other. 'Hah, this'll be apartments, mate. Bet on it. A couple of grand a month, no sweat. They know none of us are up for that so they didn't bother with the politeness.'

'Still, possible grounds for a legal challenge?' Don said. 'Cliff?'

I was watching Frank, wondering how he was going to negotiate the biscuits and cheese.

'Sure, Don,' Lucille Harvey said. 'What d'we do? Club together and get a QC?'

Somehow, Frank handled it. He's a big man with a wide mouth and he managed to absorb half of the biscuit sandwich in one bite, not many crumbs falling onto his bulging waistcoat. Frank maintains that people expect an antiquarian bookseller to wear a waistcoat. He washed the mouthful down with a slug of red. I nodded my congratulations and turned my attention to the conversation.

'Don might be right,' I said. 'And Lucille's right as well. Upshot is, we're fucked.'

Don took a cautious sip of his wine. 'Steph?'

Stephanie Geller, ruby-lipped, kohl-eyed, in a sequinned top and a long skirt festooned with tiny mirrors, was pissed. She's short-sighted and won't wear glasses because she thinks they're bad for her image. She squinted and smiled lopsidedly. 'Zee cards . . . zee cards say Cliff's right, even though he's a fuckin' sceptic's sceptic. We're fucked. Henri, get me another white.' Steph forgets the accent once in a while.

'You're drunk, darling,' Henri Baden said. Steph told me once that Henri is a con man who tells people what they want to hear. He's one of those gays that seem to get gayer by the glass.

'Don't darling me, you poofter.'

'Steph!' Lucille Harvey snarled.

It went downhill from there. Goodbye St Peters Lane, goodbye central location, goodbye cheap rent.

I was working from home and not liking it. My place in Glebe doesn't lend itself to being an office as well as a house. The front room's too small; the living space is filled with books and now holds a couple of filing cabinets. You can't escort people upstairs, not when the runner's worn and the spare room holds a bed, a computer and more books. I was reduced to meeting my clients at places of their or my choice. I was to meet Dr Elizabeth Farmer in her room in the Linguistics Department of Sydney University.

A day in early spring, clear and cool. I walked. The linguists were housed in a building that looked like a cross between a Nissan hut and a school demountable. It was probably intended to be temporary, but a creeper had grown over it, trees and shrubs crowded close and it was there to stay in all its grey, small-windowed anonymity. From what I'd heard about the way things were going at universities lately, maybe a low profile was a good thing. The bean counters and productivity assessors just might leave you alone.

It was cold in the corridor—poor insulation and inade-quate heating. It'd be an oven in summer. I found a notice telling me the number of Dr Farmer's room and tracked it down. The door was open and I heard voices coming from inside. I walked past, slowly enough to see a young female dressed like a student sitting forward in a chair and an older woman behind a desk. They kept their voices low and I couldn't catch what they were saying. Probably wouldn't have understood anyway.

I was early as usual and it was one of those times I used to fill in by smoking. Now I wandered around looking at noticeboards, passing a couple of other open doors, drifting back to Dr Farmer's room. Ten minutes past our appointed time the student hurried away, backpack over one shoulder, scarf dangling, muttering to herself. I knocked on the open door and presented myself.

She stood and beckoned to me. 'Mr Hardy. Sorry to keep you waiting.'

I went in and took the hand she extended. She was tall and well built with thick dark hair going attractively grey. I must have gaped just a bit because she laughed as she pointed to the chair. 'I know, I know. I look like Germaine Greer. No relation. I just do.'

I sat and then stood. 'Can I close the door?'

'Of course. Have you been around a university lately?'

'No. Not as a student for a long time and not otherwise for quite a bit.'

We both settled into our chairs. 'You can't be in a room with a student with the door shut—male or female. Possibility of improper conduct.'

'Jesus.'

'Absurd, isn't it? Conversely, you can't leave your door unlocked when you go to the loo in case your bag gets nicked . . . or your computer.'

I nodded and looked closely at her while also taking in details of the room in a professional fashion. Rooms can speak about character. Books, books and more books, filing cabinets, stacked folders, audio cassettes. She wore what looked like a heavy linen shirt, white, with a string of dark beads around her neck. Dark skirt. I guessed her age at around forty and her character as strong. I wondered if I was being called in on one of those university political cases where factions develop in departments, insults fly and crimes are alleged.

'Is this a university matter, Dr Farmer? I mean threats, harassment, that sort of thing?'

'Shit, no,' she said. 'Anything like that I could handle myself or go through the union. No, this is personal and nothing to do with my profession. D'you remember Prof Harkness?'

I did. Harkness was an ophthalmologist who saved the sight of a Bougainville patriot who some others patriots were trying to kill. Harkness had needed some protection up to and during the operation. 'Sure, I remember him.'

'He operated on me a little while ago. Tied up a muscle to correct a squint. I used to have to wear these thick glasses. Anyway, apparently I babbled a bit under the anaesthetic and he was interested in what I said. We talked. He suggested I get in touch with you. He sings your praises.'

'I'm glad to hear it. Anyone who could've been making a million dollars a year in Macquarie Street and doesn't impresses me. What were you babbling about, Dr Farmer?'

She paused before she answered. She was a very handsome woman, possibly well aware of it but it sat lightly on her. She had a slight frown mark between her eyebrows, probably a result of the corrected squint. Her eyes were large and grey and unwavering. 'The prof took me seriously and I hope you will as well.'

'You've got my attention.'

'It's a question of how to put it. We linguists sometimes get tongue-tied, you'd be surprised to hear. D'you play golf, Mr Hardy?'

I shook my head.

'There's a phrase—paralysis by analysis—when you think about technique so much you can't actually hit the ball. What I'm talking about is similar. I'll just have to stumble through it. I might say I want you to find out who murdered my father, but I think I know *who*. What I really want is to find out how she did it and make her pay.'

2

She might have had trouble getting started, but she'd rehearsed her story well and got it up and running smoothly. Frederick Farmer had been a successful real estate agent with offices in the western and southern suburbs, the Blue Mountains and the Illawarra. In his mid-fifties he'd sold out to one of the big franchises for several million dollars and spent the next fifteen years dabbling in the stock exchange and at his hobbies—gardening, fishing and golf. Elizabeth was his only child. His wife had died ten years ago and three years later Farmer, aged sixty-five, had married Matilda Sharpe-Tarleton, a divorcee twenty-five years younger than himself.

'She calls herself Tilly,' Elizabeth Farmer said. 'That ought to tell you something. She's about two years younger than me. Can you see me calling myself Lizzie?'

I could in fact. She was smooth-skinned and now that she was animated she looked younger and full of energy. I didn't say anything because a reply wasn't invited.

'She married him for his money and led him a merry dance.'

'In what way?'

'Tried to make him do things he was past doing—overseas trips, gym workouts, golf pro-ams. She even talked him into opening up another real estate agency when he swore he'd done with all that. She's running it now with all his capital behind her and doing very well. I know what you're going to say.'

'Don't say that. I don't know what I'm going to say, so how could you?'

She made a defensive gesture. 'I'm sorry. I'm getting worked up. The police . . .'

'I'm nothing like the police.'

'Of course. Well, they automatically thought I was a kind of poor woman's Gina Reinhart. But it's nothing like that. My father had money but not Hancock-style billions. We didn't get on particularly well and it's true that he left most of it to her. But I got some and I'm sure the will was kosher. It's not about money. It's about . . .'

I waited for the word, wondering—justice? revenge? vindication?

Suddenly she seemed deflated. She slumped back in her chair. 'I'm not sure what it's about. Call it closure.'

'It won't be closure if you turn out to be right. There'd be a trial of the person you have in mind, probably media interest, books, perhaps. Think of the Kalajzich case. You've already mentioned the Hancock circus.'

'I know, I know. Call it jealousy then. She's beautiful and rich and . . .'

I shook my head. 'You're not the type to be jealous of anyone. What's your status here, senior lecturer?'

'Associate professor.'

'You don't call yourself professor.'

'I will when I get a chair.'

'There you are. A successful career woman. I've known a few gung-ho academics like you and they all have one thing in common—when they get interested or involved in something they can't let it go. They have to *know*.'

'Prof Harkness was right,' she said. 'You're the man for the job.'

Frederick Farmer had died when his weekender at Wombarra in the Illawarra had burnt to the ground. The house wasn't new or fancy. It was an old weatherboard on ten acres that had once been mine land and later an orchard. Farmer, despite his wealth, wasn't interested in high levels of personal comfort. He experimented with varieties of flowers, fished off the rock shelf and played golf at a nearby par 59 course. According to his daughter, he was spending more and more time at the coast and less with his wife, whom he'd come to dislike.

'They investigate deaths like that pretty thoroughly,' I said. 'Especially when they produce young, rich widows.'

'Of course. But on the surface of it everything appeared straightforward. Dad drank a bit at night and slept heavily. The old joint was full of stuff just waiting to give off toxic fumes—laminex, lino, vinyl, you name it. The wiring was ancient.'

I shrugged. 'It happens.'

'Not to him. He knew houses, he'd bought and sold them all his life. He was careful. He disconnected everything before he went to bed. Turned everything off and slept with a hot water bottle.'

'What about the hot water service?'

'Chip heater. He blew out the pilot light. Always.'

'You told this to the police?'

'Yes, but they took no notice. I think as soon as they saw the scotch bottles, the old two bar radiators and the chip heater they made up their minds. They said a radiator had been left on and a curtain had blown close to it and . . . whoosh. But it's not possible.'

'What about the hot water bottle?'

'Ah. Right question. They didn't find one. I don't know how hard they looked. It wouldn't have survived the fire, but no one believed me when I said he used one. I ranted on about it and Tilly . . . Matilda said she'd persuaded him not to use it, that it was a fogey thing. She's lying. He loved his hottie.'

I liked her, I liked her honesty and the homey touches, but it sounded very thin. 'How much money are we talking about? I mean, that your father's wife inherited.'

'Oh, the house in Wahroonga, the shares, the other bits and pieces, probably close to five million. I got the Wombarra place which I'd always loved, and some shares and things like my mother's jewellery and some money she had. About three-quarters of a million.'

'Big difference.'

'Sure, but I've got a house in Newtown that I own and a job that I love. No dependants. I don't need five million. She's just got her face and her figure and her greed.'

'Your father sounds like a pretty cluey guy. How come he went for a gold-digger?'

'She's a good actress, and she only showed her true colours after she got him.'

'No pre-nuptial?'

She shook her head. 'He hated lawyers.'

'Can't say I blame him.'

'Look, I don't expect you to work miracles, but surely you can look at the reports on the fire and the medical evidence and . . . do an investigation of some kind. And you could meet her and investigate her. See who she knows, what she does. If there's anything . . . I know it sounds thin.'

'Is she hands-on in the real estate agency?'

'Oh, yes. She fancies herself a great saleswoman.'

'It so happens I'm looking for office space. Where's the agency?'

She grimaced. 'Newtown. I see her far too often.'

'I was in Darlinghurst. I wouldn't mind Newtown.'

She smiled and the animation came back. 'You'll do it?'

'I've got a feeling you'd sic Harkness onto me if I didn't.' I put one of my cards on her tidy desk. 'I'll take a look at it. Siphon off a bit of your money. Give me your number and I'll fax you a contract. You can email me some of the relevant details—addresses, dates. People involved—like your father's doctor, the police you spoke to, insurance and stuff.'

'Thank you.'

'No guarantees.'

She gave me a card with her contact details on it and we shook hands. She had a strong, cool grip and there was a faint tang of something astringent about her. Standing, she was tall, in the 180 centimetre bracket. I wondered about the no dependants. I wondered about a lot of things to do with her. I always do. People who hire private detectives aren't like the normal run. They want to know other people's secrets and they usually have some of their own, sometimes harmless, sometimes not. It makes the work interesting. Anyway, I *did* need to think about office space.

. . .

Whatever chicanery goes on inside the buildings, the grounds of Sydney University are still pleasant to walk around. I drifted up from the old linguistics building, past something new and soulless and then strolled by the Fisher Library to the new set of wide steps put in to run down to Victoria Park. There used to be a gap in the fence and a rough track up from the park worn by feet that wanted to go in the logical, short-cut direction. The authorities eventually recognised the reality and they've done a good job. In a few years the steps and rails will look as if they've always been there.

A cold breeze had got up and I was underdressed in a light jacket, shirt and jeans. Some of the students on the steps had taken a better reading on the day and wore or carried coats. They probably had umbrellas in their backpacks. Spring in Sydney.

I went down the steps and decided to walk a couple of k's around the paths. I'd neglected my gym-going lately and a brisk walk to raise a sweat might help me to re-dedicate myself. The pool wasn't open yet but pretty soon the lappers would be at it in the early morning before work and the mums and dads would be hauling the kids in for lessons at twenty bucks a half hour. I'd been taught to swim by Uncle Ian, who I realised much later was no kin but a man having an affair with my mother. It hadn't exactly been a 'chuck him in at the deep end' kind of instruction, but near enough. I got the hang of it quickly enough and survived the surf at the south end of Maroubra beach for many years. I hadn't been in the water much in recent years and I could probably do with a few lessons. Maybe, I thought, but let's not make too many good resolutions all at once.

I stepped it out around the park for half an hour with

my mind running over the few minor cases I had on hand, how much I disliked working from home, and what I had begun to think of as the enigma of Dr Elizabeth Farmer. By the time I'd walked home I felt sufficiently virtuous and energised to knuckle down to the computer and complete reports on the current cases—resolving a couple, opting out of one, putting another on a low heat backburner. I had my standard contract on file. I printed one out, found Dr Farmer's card and faxed her a copy. She'd be up for an eight hundred dollar retainer and a daily rate of four hundred, plus expenses. Nice to know she could afford it. I guessed that a nearly professor was on a pretty good screw and her inheritance wasn't peanuts. Nice to think of some of it coming my way.

After faxing I went back to the email and found that she'd sent a brief message to say that she'd assemble the information I wanted when she got home and send it through. A big plus that, an efficient client, especially one who looked like the Germaine Greer of twenty-five years ago with a cool grip developed by hitting woods or metals or irons, or whatever they call them. But I had the idea that Dr Farmer wasn't interested in male partners at golf or anything else. Just a feeling.

I was scribbling down a few points on the interview with Elizabeth Farmer, working towards drawing up a list of things to do and the order to do them in, when the phone rang. I let the answering machine pick it up.

'Mr Hardy, my name is Karatsky, Marisha Karatsky. I'm in desperate need of your help. My daughter is missing. She's only fifteen and I'm very troubled about her. I . . .'

The desperation was evident in the shakiness of her voice and the shortness of her breath. I picked up the phone.

'Hardy speaking. Try to calm down, Ms Karatsky. I know it's hard. Maybe I can help. Where are you?'

'I . . . thank you, Mr Hardy, I'm right outside, on my mobile.'

Reluctantly, I'd scribbled my home address on a few cards I'd left here and there after losing the Darlinghurst office. I said something encouraging and hung up. I went downstairs, opened the front door and ushered the woman in. She was small and dark with thin features and what my gypsy grandmother called gypsy eyes—dark and hooded with the skin below them looking bruised. Grandma Lee had them, so did I to a degree. Ms Karatsky wore a long leather coat buttoned to the neck and boots with medium heels. Her hair was a wiry tangled mass. No makeup. There were no rings on her hands and she was shaking with tension as she leaned against the wall.

'Thank you. Thank you.'

The spring wind had brought spring rain and the shoulders of her coat were wet.

'Come in and sit down. Can I get you something? Coffee? A drink?'

'I'm sorry. Have you got any cognac?'

'I've got brandy.'

'Brandy, yes, of course. Some brandy, please.'

Cheap stuff for lacing coffee, but with the wind busy outside as the light died and the rain spattered on the roof, just the thing. She took off her coat and I hung it over the stair rail. She was wearing a red silk blouse and an olive green knee-length skirt. One sleeve of the blouse was buttoned at the wrist and the other had apparently lost its button and flapped freely. Happens to me. Gold watch, light gold chain around her neck.

I got her seated in the living room after clearing some newspapers from a chair and brought in two wineglasses and the bottle. I haven't got any snifters. I poured the drinks, handed her one, pulled over a stool I use for reaching the higher bookshelves, and sat. It felt more professional than slumping into one of the saggy armchairs.

Marisha Karatsky took a good pull on the brandy and let it slide down. She didn't exactly shudder but I got the feeling she was used to something smoother. I had a slug and it tasted okay to me as the first drink of the day. But that always tastes good, whatever it is.

'Take your time and tell me what's happened.'

She told me she worked freelance as a translator, providing subtitles for German, Russian and Polish films and television programs. Her father was Polish, her mother Russian and the family had lived in East Germany before immigrating to Australia. Her daughter, Kristina, was wild and easily influenced, she said. She'd left home two months before. Her mother had traced her to a shared house in Tempe from a scribbled note she'd found in Kristina's room. She went there but the place was empty, apparently uninhabited. Neighbours said it was a house where people came and went. She hadn't contacted the police.

'It's not easy for people like me, East Germans, to deal with the police. Also, Kristina uses drugs. I want to find her but I don't want to put her in prison.'

'What about her father?' I said.

She shook her head and took another drink, as if the mention of the word needed a defence. Then she smiled, showing perfect, small white teeth in a broad, thin-lipped mouth. 'A youthful indiscretion. Nothing more.'

It sounded like a subtitle.

'Okay,' I said. 'If you can give me a photograph and description of her there's a few moves I can make. I can go to the Tempe place and ask questions. I know people who . . . monitor the sort of scene Kristina's got herself into. I can ask around and try to pick up a trace, but I probably don't have to tell you it's a dangerous world with many casualties. And this is a big country with lots of ways to lose yourself. Some of them safe, some not.'

She put her drink carefully on the floor, went across to her coat, took a manila envelope from an inside pocket and handed it to me. Inside was a photograph of a dark-haired girl heading fast towards young womanhood. She looked quite like her mother with slightly broader features and a sulky expression that was perhaps trying for sultry. It was only a waist upwards shot. She wore a black T-shirt with 'Heart Ache' printed on it in pink. Earrings, several, nose-ring, one.

'She could be beautiful,' Marisha Karatsky said, 'but she can be a devil. Do you have any children, Mr Hardy?'

Not something I talked about much but this seemed like an appropriate time. 'A daughter. I didn't raise her but we got together later. She's in America and doing okay, last I heard.'

'You are lucky. There is more information for you.'

I shook out a page of typescript. Kristina's date of birth was given, her height and weight—175 centimetres, 56 kilos—much taller but skinny like Mum—and a short list of names and places.

'Those are some of her friends and some of the places she went to. I'm not sure if they are all still . . .' she waved her hands expressively. 'Around.'

I nodded. 'What about school?'

'Ah, another reason for no police. She stopped going to school last year. The truant service can't be very good because no one has contacted me. I must tell you that she never stayed at any school very long—always absent, pretending . . . I love my daughter, Mr Hardy, and I believe she could become a successful person. She is musically talented and can dance like a thing on fire. But she is lost at the moment and I don't want for her to be lost always. Will you help me? I can pay you. I earn good money.'

'I'll be honest with you, Ms Karatsky. A resourceful young person with experienced friends can be impossible to trace—even with a fairly warm trail. In cases like this, what I do is try very hard to learn something useful very quickly. If I do, there's some hope and I ask for a retainer and a contract is signed. If not, I think it's unfair to take any money beyond the initial expenses. I'm sorry if it sounds severe, but . . .'

She rose smoothly from her chair and moved towards me and I felt impelled to stand. She gripped my upper arms, raised herself on tiptoe and kissed me on both cheeks. I felt her firm breasts press against me somewhere above my belt. She smelt slightly of brandy. There are some people you meet and forget instantly and others who make such an impact you know they'll stay with you. It's a matter of looks, voice, smell and more. It had been a long time since I'd met a woman who stamped herself on me in that way and Marisha Karatsky was just such a one.

'Not severe,' she said. 'Not at all. Thank you. Thank you very much.'

3

Two clients, two cases—well, maybe two half cases, because I didn't really expect too much to come from either of them. Still, income is income and there were interesting aspects to both matters. When I checked the email the following morning, I found that Elizabeth Farmer had come through with a mass of information as well as names and addresses. Insurance documents relating to the house, a recent pest inspection, electricity bills showing very low consumption, her father's note rejecting a bottled gas offer and newspaper clippings on her father's career as a real estate agent and minor property developer. Frederick Farmer had obviously been a pretty shrewd customer who, without setting the world on fire, had built a prosperous business and sold out at the right time.

The only false note was the wedding coverage in the *Sun-Herald* of seven years back. Elizabeth must have got her good looks from her mother, because Fred was no oil painting. At sixty-five he was balding, slightly stooped from what had been a good height, and his nose and jowls betrayed the habitual heavy drinker. For all that, he looked vigorous and happy, if slightly embarrassed by the frilly

shirt and tux. Happy with good reason. Matilda Sharpe-
Tarleton was a stately blonde, elegant in a sheath dress with
discreet jewellery and accessories. Low key in a way, but
nothing could tone down the effect of her cheekbones,
swan-neck and lissom figure. She was a beautiful woman,
perhaps just past her prime but not letting go one milli-
metre. Diet, aerobics, massage, anti-oxidants.

'Viagra,' I said to myself as I looked at the photograph
again.

Dr Farmer had provided the names and phone numbers
of her father's doctor and lawyer, the insurance assessor of
her claim for the fire at what had become her property, and
the Wollongong detective who'd headed the enquiry until
Farmer's death had been pronounced accidental by the
Coroner. I checked the dates and found that the whole
thing had been wrapped up pretty quickly. Couldn't ask
for a better briefing, and it all indicated how serious she
was and therefore how seriously I should take the case. Had
to take precedence over Ms Karatsky with the gypsy eyes
and, as I made that decision, I felt regret. Not that I like
looking for teenage runaways particularly, I just liked the
gypsy eyes.

I'd decide later how to play it—give them a day at
a time, or move between the two cases as circumstances
dictated. It'd be partly a matter of geography probably.
I reread the material Elizabeth had forwarded until I was
thoroughly familiar with it. It's a good rule to start at
the top. I picked up the phone and called the Matilda
S-T Farmer real estate agency in Newtown. I gave the
person who answered a fictitious name and said I was interested in renting office space in Newtown and possibly
buying some property.

'I'm sure one of our people can help you, Mr Lees. I—'

'No,' I said, trying to sound as abrupt and objectionable as possible. 'I prefer to deal with principals. I'd like to speak to Ms Farmer.'

The temperature dropped but I got the result I wanted. 'Please give me your number, sir, and I'll have Mrs Farmer ring you when she's free.'

She rang ten minutes later. Throaty voice, careful vowels, cool tone. I got an appointment for eleven thirty, two hours away. Time for me to iron a shirt, brush my suit, get a haircut.

Newtown has changed dramatically since I first moved to the inner west. Then it was rough, grubby, neglected, now it's gentrified, clean, well-tended—a lot of it anyway. King Street has restaurants offering the cuisine of most of the nations of the world, coffee bars with internet facilities, health food stores and natural therapists, all with advertised websites. I was a little early and I wandered, looking for signs of the bad old days, but I found few. The Hub theatre looked in need of work and was up for lease; a few money-lenders suggested something other than universal affluence. But the bookshops and recycled clothing stores talked the language of now. Posters for the Enmore Theatre announced rock groups I'd never heard of. Not surprising. The Stones played there a while back, but the posters must have been souvenired.

Matilda Farmer's place of business was a surprise. It was in a huge terrace a stone's throw from the main drag. No shopfront window advertising properties, no metre-high signs. A discreet notice attached to a wrought iron fence out front and a brass plaque beside the front door and that was it. If you knew the address you could find it, if you didn't, you'd struggle. A novel approach. I began to suspect Tilly of having brains, or good advice, or both.

I went up the sandstone steps and through the open door. A buzzer sounded. The ground floor had been gutted to the back wall, leaving a large space for a modern-looking office with a number of desks, computers, faxes, photocopiers—the works. Five people working the computers and phones. Three others with real live clients at their desks. The stairs to the upper levels were wide with a handsomely polished handrail. The lighting was subdued and the ceiling roses were intact, ditto a couple of marble fireplaces. I got the idea: if you were looking to buy and restore but keep the Victorian charm, this was the place to shop.

A sleek young woman sitting at the front desk rose smoothly and gave me a sceptical smile. My suit might've been brushed but it wasn't Italian.

'Can I help you?'

I handed her a card that said I was Gerard Lees, Security Consultant. It gave my address as the defunct office in Darlinghurst. A check would confirm my story of needing office space. 'Mr Lees to see Mrs Farmer. I have an appointment.'

She recognised the name. This was the woman I'd spoken to on the phone. She hadn't liked me then and she wasn't about to change her mind. She avoided looking at me altogether.

'This way, please.'

We went up the stairs. Figured. The boss lady wouldn't be down at ground level with the peasants. My guide tapped at a door that was standing ajar.

'Mr Lees, Mrs Farmer.'

The easily identifiable voice said, 'Yes. Show him in. Coffee in five, Phoebe.'

The newspaper photographs hadn't done her justice. In them she looked pampered but in the flesh she looked harder, more resilient. Less beautiful, perhaps, than when tricked out for her wedding, but handsome and arresting. She glided around her desk and held out her hand.

'Mr Lees. Glad to meet you.'

A firm, businesslike shake.

'Mrs Farmer. I have to say I'm a little worried about your security—that open door.'

'Take a seat, and don't worry. It all locks up tight enough at night. There's a concealed camera running twenty-four hours a day with a hook-up to a security firm. Plus one of those men downstairs is a highly trained—'

I held up a hand. 'Okay, okay, I'm convinced. Anyway, I don't want you to get the wrong idea. I'm buying, not selling.'

'Good.'

'I haven't been in Newtown for quite some time. It's changed.'

'For the better, I'm sure. Ah, here's the coffee.'

Quick five minutes. Maybe Phoebe knew five meant two. After the coffee routine, Matilda quizzed me about my needs and I cooked up a story that had some elements of the truth. The rent I said I was prepared to pay was pure fiction. She reeled off a list of places that might suit, referring only occasionally to the computer. She pretty much had the information down pat. I hummed and hawed a bit and then said I was impressed by her place of business and wondered if I could get something like it. Perhaps combine office and home.

She smiled, and for the first time I saw something of the shark in her expression. Just a flash. You didn't need a realtor's licence to know that the real money was in big terraces in almost any condition as long as they had walls and a roof.

'It's a sound idea,' she said. 'I have an apartment here on the upper level and I find it very convenient. As an investment, property in Newtown can scarcely be beaten.'

I nodded. 'I like the idea. Somewhere at the hub, like here and maybe something on the coast. Have you got a weekender, Mrs Farmer? If you don't mind me asking.'

'No, not at present. But I have my eye on some land.'

Personal stuff over, we got down to details and she made me some appointments—none of which I intended to keep—to look at office space and roomy houses with the potential to double as work and home. Super efficient, she tapped keys and printed me out a sheet with the appointment details—times and addresses—and the names of what she called her 'associates'.

I didn't have to pretend to be impressed. I was. It struck me that she enjoyed every element of what she was doing. The ash blonde hair, drawn severely back, came slightly loose and she flicked it away without worrying about it. Her makeup didn't conceal the encroaching lines around her eyes and mouth and wasn't intended to. She wore a dark suit with a V-necked silk top under it that showed off the smooth column of her neck. No lines there to speak of.

We finished our business and she stood and extended her hand again. 'Where are you from, Mr Lees?'

I gave her my try at an enigmatic smile. The one that went with the broken nose and the hooded eyes and that, depending on the circumstances, can look dumb or desperate. 'Why?'

'Don't be offended. These days, one has to be careful. I have to tell you that a corporate client renting property through me has to go through a security check. Not stringent, but . . .'

I laughed. 'You think I look like an Arab, is that it?'

She didn't answer.

'I'm mostly Irish, Mrs Farmer. And not IRA—not at all, at all.'

I went away with the cards of a few of the agency's representatives in my pocket and a fair degree of confusion in my mind. Elizabeth Farmer's portrayal of what I supposed should be called her stepmother seemed wildly inaccurate. Matilda Farmer was no empty-headed gold-digger but a shrewd, well-organised and capable businesswoman. She fancies herself a super saleswoman, Elizabeth had said. That was wrong. She was that without a doubt and possibly something more.

The indications were that the business was doing well. The injection of a few million dollars would have set it solidly on its feet, but it was nothing like a hobby or vanity affair or a tax dodge. Not that my assessment really changed anything. Elizabeth's judgement that Matilda had Frederick Farmer murdered for his money only needed a slight readjustment to read: for his money and control of a business she knew she could turn into a gold mine. Central was the question of Matilda's character—the purpose of my visit. I had my own opinion now, rating the woman pretty highly. Ruthless, though? Quite possibly.

I called into the pub on the corner of King Street and Missenden Road, just up from the hospital. It had been thoroughly revamped since I'd last been there, when it was a hangout for locals including the residents of the many boarding houses in the area, boxers and footballers from the two gyms nearby, and people visiting friends and relatives in the hospital and thanking God they could get away. Now it was all carpet and muted light with pinball and slot machines and red wine at five dollars a glass.

I sat on a stool and looked out through a tinted window at the street. As I watched, a Camry station sedan slipped into a parking space about twenty metres away. Elizabeth Farmer got out from the driver's side and another woman from the passenger side. She was younger, smaller and blonde, wearing a knee-length suede coat, black slacks and high-heeled boots. The two women linked arms and set off down the street.

One question answered, quite a few still to go.

4

Tempe was only a couple of kilometres away and I decided to take a look at the house where the missing Kristina had stayed. Sharing suggests paying rent and how does a fifteen-year-old get money to pay rent? A few ways I could think of, all tricky and all likely to leave a trail. I skipped lunch in the interest of my waistline, hauled out the trusty *Gregory's*, and located the address Ms Karatsky had given me.

The street was a narrow dead-ender with the traffic roar of the Princes Highway as a backdrop. The houses were small and tightly packed; a few had had the renovator's wand waved over them but most hadn't. Ten years ago, rents would have been cheap and there would probably have been squats in this area—houses from deceased estates left to rot, or places where rising damp and decayed roofs had driven out owners and renters. Now the semis and narrow, freestanding houses were all occupied with the residents on mortgages or paying hefty rents. Position, position, position—you could get to the CBD in lots of ways from here. Sydney being Sydney, many of the people had driven their cars. No off-street parking. Oil stains in the vacant spots showed that the street would be solidly parked on both sides at night. Outside number 12, the place I was interested in, were plenty of oil stains but no vehicle.

Number 12 was a faded brick semi with a gap-toothed wrought iron fence and an overgrown scrap of front garden. A peppercorn tree, sprouting slantwise from behind the fence, hung high and bushy over the footpath, reaching almost to the gutter. Pedestrians would have to brush the branches aside to get by. Bad news for joggers and I was sure there'd be some around these parts.

I pushed open the sagging gate and went up a weed-broken path and some well-worn steps to the narrow porch in front of the house. None of your fancy tiling here; this place had gone up when austerity was the go. There were bars on the windows and a solid security screen. I pressed the buzzer and took out my PEA licence folder and the photograph of Kristina. A barefoot young woman in jeans and T-shirt opened the door and stood behind the screen.

I explained my business, showed her the ID and the photograph.

'Yeah, she was here. Next door told us about her mum but we weren't home.'

'And she told me. Could I come in, please?'

She wiped the back of her hand across her nose and sniffed. 'Why?'

'I thought perhaps I could have a look in the room she had. See if she left anything behind.'

'She didn't.'

'I mean a professional look. Could be something you missed.'

'You're a real private eye, right?'

'Yep.'

She unlatched the screen door. 'Suppose it's all right. I love those movies. You see *Chinatown*?'

'Many times.'

'Me too. Come in, Mr . . . ?'

I showed her the folder again as I edged inside. 'Hardy. And you are . . . ?'

'Denise. Kristina had the second room off to the left. Harry's in there now and it's full of his shit, so you probably won't find anything.'

'Just a quick look, then.'

She padded down the threadbare carpet behind me. I stood aside and let her open the door. The smell from inside nearly knocked me back against the wall. Denise grinned and sniffed again. 'I've gotta cold. I'll get a tissue.'

The smell was made up of tobacco, marijuana, sweat and dirty socks. Harry, whoever he was, dropped his clothes where he stood, liked his window closed and his sheets stiff. Denise was right, there could be no trace of a previous occupant in here. I was backing out when I heard a shout from the front door.

'Denise, how many fuckin' times have I told you to keep that fuckin' screen locked?'

Denise was back, dabbing at her nose. 'Sorry, Harry.'

'Sorry, Harry,' he mocked. 'Who the fuck's this you've let in, you silly cunt?'

Harry was big, 190 centimetres plus, going on a hundred kilos, some of it blubber, not all. He had a shaven head and his jeans, T-shirt and bomber jacket looked to be in much the same condition as the clothes on the floor in his room. He loomed in the narrow hallway like a Mack truck in a one-way street. I knew the type—his size had won him most of his fights before they even started.

He pushed Denise away savagely when she made a placatory move towards him and that was enough for me. Our relative heights were just right. I put my left shoulder hard into his sternum and gave him a solid right to the ribs at the same time. Double whammy. The fight and the breath went out of him in a long whoosh. It wasn't too hard to hit him again with the shoulder and send him crumbling down like a deflated windsock. Denise's eyes were wide open. She'd never seen Harry outplayed before. I made a gesture to show her that I'd finished and crouched down beside Harry who was gasping for breath.

'Keep your day job, mate, whatever it is. You'll never make it as a tough guy. Now, I intended to be polite about this but you changed the rules. I'm going to ask some questions and you're going to answer them if you want to keep your teeth.' I put a fist under his nose. 'Understand?'

He nodded.

'Did Kristina leave anything behind in the room? Anything at all?'

Another nod.

'What?'

'C . . . card.'

'Where is it?'

He squirmed and reached around for his wallet in his hip pocket. I'd felt something give when the rib punch landed. He was hurting. He fumbled a card out of the wallet and I took it. It was for a brothel in Alexandria— 'The Silken Touch'—with the usual graphic: couches, tresses, diaphanous gowns. On the back of it was scrawled, 'Anytime—K.'

'Going to pay her a visit, were you?'

Denise had seen the card. 'You bastard,' she said.

I straightened up. 'Okay, sorry to upset the domestic harmony here. A few more questions. Why did she leave?'

Denise said, 'She was dealing and using. We kicked her out.'

'When was this?'

Denise shrugged. 'A week.'

'And she hasn't been back?'

She shot Harry an evil look. 'Not as far as I know.'

'All right.' I gave her one of my cards. 'You have any trouble with this bloke you call me. Okay?'

'Okay.' Her cold seemed to have gone and I had the feeling Harry would follow it soon. I gave him a pat on his bald head and left the house.

Three o'clock in the afternoon is as good a time as any to go calling at a brothel. They operate around the clock and the manager or an assistant would be there and at least some of the workers. Kristina struck me as a night-time gal, but you never know. Most of these places have some kind of protection, and the protector wasn't likely to be such easy meat as Harry. I stopped at an ATM along the way and drew out some money.

The Silken Touch was in Botany Road with no danger of offending churchgoers or schoolchildren. It was behind a high wall with the number painted on it, large enough for there to be no mistake about punters coming to the right place. There was a factory on one side and a warehouse of some kind on the other; blocks of flats opposite.

I parked and pressed the buzzer beside a heavy metal gate. A mounted security camera above the gate would have shown them inside that I probably wasn't an axe murderer and definitely not a Jehovah's Witness. The gate swung smoothly in and I stepped through and along a short covered walkway to the front of the building. It looked like a Federation house that had undergone more renovation than Michael Jackson. The front porch had been glassed in, a bow window flattened and a bullnose verandah re-modelled. Every bit of glass in view was tinted and every surface had a fresh coat of paint.

The front door opened at a touch and I stood in a dis-creetly lit reception area where a woman sat behind a desk. There were chairs for clients, a flat screen television, a VCR, a rack of videos and magazines and prints on the walls that advertised what was on sale here. The woman remained seated. She was a redhead, at least for now, with a wide, flat face, strong jaw and an oddly small mouth. She wore a rollneck sweater with a heavy gold chain hanging between her impressive breasts.

'Good afternoon, sir.' Careful vowels and consonants, a small smile from the small mouth, a semi-welcoming gesture of the hands.

'Good afternoon. I'm not a client. I'd like to speak to whoever's in charge here.'

That announcement changed her manner in an instant. She pressed a button on her desk. A door opened behind her and a man came striding towards us. White shirt, dark pants, no tie. He was medium-sized, short-haired and fluid in his movement. Army-trained if ever I saw it.

I took out my licence folder and the photograph of Kristina along with three one hundred dollar notes which I held so that he could see them and the woman at the desk couldn't.

'Help you, mate?'

'Somewhere we can talk?'

He had good eyes; he'd seen the money and taken in the details of the licence. 'I'll handle this, Phyllis. Come through here, Mr Hardy.'

I gave Phyllis a wink and followed him past a series of blown-up photographs showing black men and white women and white men and black women, proving, I suppose, that opposites can attract. He opened a door into a room containing a desk and chair and a three-quarter bed. A screen mounted so it could be seen from the bed showed a movie with the sound turned down. Two women with silicone pumped breasts were seesawing on a double dildo. Another screen, placed to be viewed from behind the desk, was blank but with a faint glimmer. He saw me notice it.

'The camera's heat-activated. The latest.'

'Cute,' I said. 'You know my name. What's yours?'

'Phil. Now, what's this about?'

I'm no great shakes at sleight of hand but I can do a bit when needed. I made the money disappear and handed him the photograph.

'D'you know this girl, Phil?'

'If I do?'

'Could be trouble. She's young.'

'How young?'

'That depends.'

'What's this? Some kind of shakedown?'

'A nice kind. You tell me everything you know about her and you walk away with the money and that's it. If you don't do that there could be . . . consequences.'

'I could hurt you.'

'You could. Army?'

'Right.'

'Me too, but a fair while ago. I'd back you in, but why take the risk?'

He thought about it the way a man who enjoys violence does. Dumb ones go for it no matter what, smarter ones pick their moments. 'Okay, I know the girl. Calls herself Kristina. Looks a lot older than in that photo, though.'

'You would say that, wouldn't you? I don't suppose she's around now?'

He shook his head.

'When?'

'What's the date?'

I told him.

'Next week, the tenth. She was here two days, then said she was taking a week off. They come and go. They're free agents. Plenty around.'

'Did she . . . give satisfaction?'

He shrugged. 'Far as I know.'

'Out calls or here?'

'Both.'

'Her address?'

'No, and we haven't got her ABN or her tax file number or her—'

'Okay, I get the picture. You must have some way of getting in touch. Mobile?'

He nodded. The terse type.

'Give me that for real and you've got your money and I'm gone.'

'How do I know you won't raise a stink anyway?'

'How do I know you won't come after me and have a go?'

'Fair enough.' He went to the desk, pulled out a drawer

and consulted a notebook. He read off the numbers and I scribbled them down. I handed him the money.

'Sure you don't want to stay a while? Some pretty hot babes here.'

'I'm too old for hot, I prefer cool.'

'Suit yourself.' He pocketed the money and turned his attention back to the television. The sound came up—the usual pulsing rhythm and heavy breathing plus squeals.

'One more thing—was she a junkie?'

He kept his eyes on the television. 'No way. No tracks and we do a fair dinkum blood test.'

Interesting. Not exactly good news to tell her mother given the source, but something.

Things were slow, just Phyllis in reception, no takers, no givers. I nodded to her and got a stony stare in reply. I went out, unshipped my mobile and rang the number as I leaned against the car.

'The mobile phone you have called is either switched off or cannot be reached at this time. Please call again later.'

5

Standing probably twenty metres away from him, I rang Phil and gave him the news about Kristina's mobile number. I told him that I'd keep trying to contact Kristina, but that if I didn't reach her he should ring me the minute she turned up. He didn't like it but, with the way things were with public, media and police interest in the underage sex scene, he didn't have much choice. A white Commodore pulled up as I was driving away—business at last.

I didn't have anything much to report to either of my clients, but the day hadn't been a complete zero. I drove around aimlessly for a while, just letting impressions form and take shape. I drifted back towards Glebe, going with the flow of the mid-afternoon traffic. The twin towers in New York might be gone, but the two towers of the Tempe brickworks still stood, although the huge rubbish dump and quarry have been landscaped into something called, with brilliant imagination, Sydney Park. I made a mental note to have a good walk around its rolling grassy hectares some day. Perhaps jog around it. Perhaps.

Old habits die hard, especially those associated with work. I've heard of writers who couldn't tap out a word for months after giving up smoking or going off the grog. I was still coming to terms with having no office to go to—no way to break up the day, compartmentalise life and work. I'd always done a certain amount of work at home—read files, made phone calls, used the computer—but having only the house as a base irked me. I'd liked the vibe of Darlinghurst—the number of people there living on the edge, taking risks, bombing out, occasionally coming up trumps. It acted as an antidote to the conformity I felt creeping over the country, seeping out from the conservative mandarins of Canberra. The upshot was that, increasingly, with no office to go to I didn't want to go home.

I keep a spare set of clothes, a toothbrush and shaving gear in the car for those times when it's not possible to go home. This time it was a matter of choice. With the Kristina Karatsky case on hold and possibly headed for a win, there was no reason not to scoot down to the south coast and take a look at the burnt-out house in Wombarra. I'd taken notes from the stuff Elizabeth Farmer had given me so I knew the names of the people I needed to talk to. I hit the Princes Highway and went south.

I hadn't been to the Illawarra in some time but I remembered the lie of the land pretty well. You leave the highway south of Waterfall if you want the coast road, otherwise you stick on it all the way to the Bulli Pass. I'm like most Australians, the coast has a special appeal for me, and I remembered the coastline south from Stanwell Tops as spectacular. A tonic to an old surfer. I got a greatest hits station on the radio and settled back to enjoy the drive once I'd got past the used car yards and auto accessory supermarkets. The Eagles and Credence were good company and at Heathcote the Beach Boys felt like a bonus.

I swung left down towards Stanwell Park and the plan came unstuck. A flashing sign above the road read: COAST ROAD CLOSED AT COALCLIFF. The narrow road carved into the cliff with a straight drop to the sea is fragile. Signs in this area read 'Falling Rocks Do Not Stop' and they don't. I swore and drove down as far as the turnoff just to get a glimpse of the coastline before u-turning and heading back to the highway.

It was after five when I got to Bulli where I stopped for petrol. The young attendant was a livewire who insisted on checking the oil, water and tyres. He found a soft one and gave it some air. The process took longer than it usually does and, with daylight saving still a couple of weeks away, the light was dropping and it would be even darker at Wombarra, four towns back in the shadow of the escarpment. I drove to Thirroul and checked into the motel where Brett Whiteley had cashed in his chips. If it had been America they would've tricked out his room and charged a special rate. Not so here. It was a quiet time with plenty of vacancies. I might've been in Brett's room, not that I cared one way or the other.

It hadn't been strenuous, but, with the deception at Matilda Farmer's office, the aggro in Tempe, the progress in Alexandria and the miles covered, it felt like a full day. I ate a passable meal in one of the town's restaurants, bought a bottle of white and took it back to the room where I watched television for a while, read a bit from one of the many paperbacks lying around in the car, and was asleep by 11 pm.

I woke up a few times and thought I could hear the waves of the Tasman Sea hitting the Illawarra shore. I was probably too far back to really hear it, but imagining it was just as good. An orange juice from the mini-bar and two cups of instant coffee did for breakfast. I put on my gym gear that I also keep in the car and went for a jog down to the beach and along the sand. Pretty nice beach at Thirroul and the surfers were already out. Still in their wetsuits, though. I thought about a swim, decided against it. The tiled and chlorinated saltwater pool was open and there was no entrance fee. With Sydney only an hour and a bit away by train, it was a pretty good place to live. I had a memory of some famous literary figure hanging around here for a spell and writing about the place, and the name jumped out at me—D. H. Lawrence. I remembered the name of the book, *Kangaroo*. I'd never read it; hadn't read much of him at all apart from *Lady Chatterley's Lover* when we were finally allowed. A bit dull, I thought.

My change of clothes amounted to jeans, a flannie, a T-shirt and a pair of sandals I'd picked up in New Caledonia the year before. There was still a nip in the air so I put the flannie on over the T-shirt until the day warmed up. Good south coast outfit. I paid my bill with my always stretched Amex card, and drove north to Wombarra. The next town up was Austinmer which has a long history as a beach holiday spot, and then Coledale and Wombarra, both mining towns in the old days, and now more or less dormitory suburbs for Sydney and Wollongong commuters.

I keep a selection of directories for different areas—Wollongong, Newcastle, the Blue Mountains—in the car for out-of-town jobs. The address Dr Farmer had given me was for a road running parallel to the railway line and well above it. I took the steep turnoff at Coledale and made the climb with the old Falcon performing well. The escarpment seemed to loom just above the road although in fact it was still a good way back. House numbers were hard to spot. Some of the houses were weekenders. The owners didn't get much mail here and didn't bother to keep the numbers clear of bushes and trees. Eventually I worked out which was the Farmer block by a process of elimination.

It was narrow-fronted and seemed to run back a long way in a sort of fan shape. The grass in front of the fence was overgrown and the wide gate leading to a track was padlocked. I got out of the car and shivered. Tall trees to the east blocked the sun and the area was clinging to its night-time chill. I exchanged the sandals for socks and sneakers and approached the gate. The land on the other side of the road looked unoccupied and the nearest neighbour was a hundred metres away to the right. The Farmer land was bounded to the north by a narrow street running down to the railway.

I climbed the gate and walked down the driveway. The grass at the sides and in the middle had grown back aggressively, indicating that no vehicles had passed by recently. The track bent south. The place was giving off an air of neglect but that didn't concern the healthy stand of trees fifty metres down. A horticultural ignoramus, even I could tell when flame trees and jacarandas have been deliberately planted and cared for. I passed through the red and purple display, pushing through spider webs, and saw where the house had been. Perfect spot. The land dropped away to the north-east and gaps in the trees gave a glimpse of the water in the near distance. What had been garden and lawn all around was a weed field, and only blackened stumps and a crumbling brick chimney remained of the house.

I walked through the knee-high grass soaking the legs of my jeans, socks and sneakers. I spent some time as an insurance investigator many years ago and knew what to look for when arson was suspected, but you have to be on the spot while the embers are still warm to learn anything useful. This site had been rained on, windblown, shat on by birds, rooted through by animals. No trace of anything dodgy could remain. Still, you can learn something about the former occupants even from a ruin like this. Indications were that virtually no renovation had ever been done to what was originally a fairly large fibro cottage. The rooms were small, suggesting pre-World War II construction. The back verandah, which would have afforded a glimpse of the water, hadn't been built in to provide extra living or sleeping space. The only signs of recent maintenance were the bits of guttering lying around. Thoroughly blackened, but no rust.

Dr Farmer had said the house was heated by bar radiators, so evidently the combustion stove, blackened and rusty, still standing under the chimney, had been inoperative. Pity, nothing better than heating up the kitchen on a cold country morning by getting the stove going. I remembered holidays in Katoomba with friends of my parents and my city-dwelling father clumsily wielding the axe and hatchet to get the kindling and stove wood. Everything cooked was fried and tasted terrific . . .

'What the hell d'you think you're doing?'

The voice came from a woman who'd approached from the south side without me hearing her. Too busy reminiscing. She was tall and slender in a heavy sweater, corduroy pants and gumboots. Her hair was dark with grey streaks glinting in the sunlight filtering through the tops of the trees. She carried the sort of stick I should have had for pushing away the cobwebs and she looked capable of using it for other purposes.

'I'm working for Dr Elizabeth Farmer,' I said.

'Is that right? Can you prove it?'

'Perhaps you should tell me why you've got the right to ask.'

She picked her way sure-footedly through the charred ruins and stopped within a metre of me. 'I live over behind this property. She . . . Elizabeth asked me to see if the orchard could be revived.'

I reached into my wallet, took out Dr Farmer's card and showed it to her. I said, 'She didn't mention you to me.'

'Cards don't prove anything.'

'I've got a mobile in the car. You can ring her and check.'

She looked at me closely. She had strong, symmetrical features, slightly weathered skin, capable-looking hands one side or the other of forty. We realised simultaneously that each was examining the other and we both saw the humour of it. Her grin brought a small network of lines and wrinkles in her face to life. 'I suppose you could be telling the truth,' she said. 'What're you doing for Elizabeth?'

I showed her my licence folder and told her. That changed her manner completely.

'Bloody hell, it's about time. I'm glad to hear it. I'm Sue Holland.'

We shook hands. 'Cliff Hardy.' I flipped the folder closed. 'I take it you think the fire here wasn't an accident?'

'Fred? Burn his house down? No chance.'

'He was getting on. Maybe he just slipped up a bit and . . .'

She shook her head. 'No way. I saw him that day. Sharp as a tack, old Fred. Pissed off at that wife of his as usual, but not dotty.'

'We'd better have a proper talk, ah, Ms, Mrs . . .'

'Sue. Where's your car?'

I pointed and she told me to drive down the street beside the Farmer property and come in where I saw a two metre high stump with the name Holland painted on it. I did as instructed and followed a track for close to a hundred metres, finishing up at a sandstone cottage in a rainforest clearing. I waited and Sue who-had-to-be Holland came tramping through the bush to the side of the cottage. She snapped her stick across her knee and threw the three pieces onto a woodheap under a galvanised iron lean-to. Smoke was rising from a chimney at the rear of the house and she gestured to me to come back there.

'Come in. The front of the place is freezing. I live out the back until the summer.'

I followed her along a gravel path to a set of brick steps where she kicked off her boots. She gave a sharp whistle and an old dog came slowly out of a kennel near the steps. She patted his head and murmured something to him.

'Poor old feller,' she said. 'He used to come with me everywhere but now he can barely raise a trot. Come on in. D'you drink tea or coffee?'

'Coffee. Thanks. What's his name?'

She glanced sharply at me. 'Why?'

I shrugged. 'Just asking. I like dogs and wish I could have one but my lifestyle doesn't allow it.'

'Oh, I thought you were being prescient. His name's Fred. I named him after Elizabeth's dad when I got him from the pound.' She laughed. 'Cunning dog, he was older than he looked.'

We went into the kitchen where a combustion stove very like the one I remembered from Katoomba was heating the space nicely. Tiled floor with a few rugs, pine table with chairs, workbenches, two tall pine dressers, old style sink, new style fridge and microwave. She hefted a big black kettle over to the sink and ran the tap. She dumped it on the stove, opened the hinged door and stirred up the fire, fed in some light wood.

'Won't be long. I could use the jug but I prefer it this way.'

'I would too.'

'You don't strike me as a country type.'

'I'm not. Boyhood memories and romantic fantasies.'

'Have a seat.' She busied herself spooning ground coffee and getting mugs down from the dresser. The draining board on the sink was empty. She was compulsive about putting things away, like me. I sat at the table and enjoyed watching her as she went unselfconsciously about the tasks, padding softly across the tiles in her thick socks. The kettle whistled and she poured the water and set the plunger.

'Milk?'

'If you've got it. Doesn't matter.'

We settled with two steaming mugs of coffee and about a hundred years of pine table history between us. The surface was scarred and scorched and gouged, but it had been oiled and cared for lately and gave off a soft, yellow gleam.

She saw me noticing. 'This was the mine manager's house. The shaft entrance is about fifty metres off that-away.' She pointed. 'Covered with lantana now, of course.'

I nodded and drank some of the very good coffee. 'I didn't expect anything like this.'

'Like what?'

'Someone so knowledgeable about the area and about the Farmers. Lucky.'

She shrugged. 'Don't know what good it'll do you. What's your brief from Elizabeth?'

I sipped. 'You're very direct.'

'I don't like to piss about. I know Elizabeth thinks Matilda hyphen whatever had Fred killed. I think it's likely but no one else does. What are you supposed to do, prove it?'

'Investigate,' I said.

'Oh, right—sit on the fence and charge so much a day.'

I drank more coffee and said nothing.

She cupped her hands around the mug. 'I'm sorry. That was rude and offensive. It's just that she needs someone on her side.'

'You are.'

'Apart from me. I can do bugger-all. Have you met Matilda?'

'Yes.'

'What d'you reckon?'

I liked this woman. I liked her house and her dog. I liked her coffee and the way the flue in her combustion stove didn't work perfectly so that there was a bit of fragrant wood smoke in the kitchen. 'I'd say she was capable of almost anything.'

'Good on you. More coffee?'

6

Sue Holland was a lecturer in horticulture at Wollongong TAFE. She'd bought the mine manager's cottage on three hectares ten years before when she'd got the job, using an inheritance and taking out a solid mortgage. She was divorced, no children. She'd got to know Frederick Farmer and Elizabeth some years before his first wife's death.

'They came down together pretty often,' she said. 'I didn't see much of him at first when he married Matilda and then I saw him a lot—after that went sour. We got on well. He was a nice man. Loved the bush.'

We were on our second mug of coffee and the kitchen had heated up. I wanted to take off the flannel shirt but worried that it'd look presumptuous. I wiped away some perspiration and she laughed. 'Heats up in here, doesn't it?' She stripped off her sweater. She wore a loose, collarless white cotton shirt under it. 'Better take off the flannie. I've got things to tell you.'

I took the shirt off and draped it over the back of my chair. I'd tucked my notebook into the hip pocket of my jeans and I pulled it out. 'Got a pen?'

She found one near the phone and passed it to me.

'I saw someone hanging around Fred's house a couple of times in the week before the fire. I didn't think much of it. There's all sorts of council types—inspectors, dog catchers. I told the police and would've given evidence at the inquest but it was over before I knew about it. The cops were useless. They didn't like Elizabeth and they don't like me.'

I'd made a note. I looked at her.

'Dykes,' she said.

'I'd have thought enlightenment would have penetrated this far south.'

'Nothing much penetrates the skull of Detective Sergeant Barton of Bellambi.'

'I know the type.'

'I told him about the . . . lurker. He thinks I'm a man-hater, which I'm not, and he thinks Matilda's shit doesn't smell.'

I poised the pen. 'Can you tell me exactly what you saw and when, with dates if you can recall them? Did you see a car? Describe the person as precisely as you can. Did he leave anything behind? I want impressions, guesses, anything you can rake up.'

She smiled. 'You're as different from Barton as it's possible to be.'

'Thanks. He's on my list of people to see. Do you know someone called Carson Lucas?'

'Is anyone called Carson Lucas?'

'The insurance investigator, I'm told.'

'Never met him.'

'It doesn't sound as if the thing was gone into very closely.'

'Right.'

'That's strange. Usually—'

'You have to understand how things are down here. Local matters determine the thinking and the action. Fred had an offer for his place. Good offer, but he turned it down. Me too. Has to be a developer, even though the area can't be subdivided. But the pressure builds and zoning can be changed. The council is keen to get more ratepayers. The cops want more paved roads, gutters, street lights, fewer secluded acres where people can grow dope, cook up speed . . .'

'You're giving me more suspects than Matilda.'

'What if she was in with them?'

'You're a conspiracy theorist.'

'You bet. You don't think the conquest of Iraq was conspired at?'

'Big scale, that.'

'The scale doesn't matter—the principle's the same. Follow the money.'

'You're teaching me my job.'

'I think you already know it.'

We talked for a little while longer. She gave me as accurate a description of the person she'd seen as she could. It wasn't much—small to medium and carrying a clipboard—hence her guess at an official. Raincoat. It had been raining both times, and then she came up with the sort of thing that makes my job hard but interesting.

'I was nearly a hundred metres away both times,' she said. 'Buggering around among the old apple and pear trees. There was just something about him that struck me as odd. Sorry, can't put my finger on it. Look, I'd had a joint, one of those times. It can sharpen you up, or, you know . . .'

I knew, although more about the effect of whisky than marijuana. I got her phone number and gave her my card. I thanked her for the coffee and the information.

'No worries. How's Elizabeth?'

I thought about it. 'Composed.'

'That'd be right. She with anyone?'

I shrugged. 'I saw her at the uni.'

I didn't like to lie to her, but gossip wasn't my game. We shook hands again and I patted Fred on the head on the way to my car. He barely stirred.

I drove back to Thirroul and had a swim in the beachside pool. The water was cold but after a few laps I didn't feel it and stayed at it long enough to feel I'd had a reasonable workout. I showered and changed back into the clothes I'd worn the day before. The shirt wasn't the freshest, but the outfit looked better for calling on cops and insurance officers than the flannie and jeans. I wondered why Elizabeth Farmer hadn't told me about the development angle. Possibly because she wanted Matilda to be at the bottom of everything. Not very objective, but that tends to happen with fallings-out inside families.

The Bellambi police station was next to the courthouse on the highway, both solid old structures reflecting an investment in law and order. I went through the door of the cop shop and got what I expected—an old shell, new fittings. Air conditioning, computers, bulletin boards bristling with pinned-up papers. An outer office for the uniforms and civilian support staff and an inner sanctum for the detectives. A fresh-faced young constable left his desk and approached the chest-high counter. Counters in police stations are always higher than elsewhere. Don't know why. Must ask.

'Yes, sir?'

I showed him my licence folder, let him discover that I had clean fingernails and didn't smell of alcohol and asked to see Sergeant Barton. For a minute I thought he was going to get me to fill in a form, but he didn't.

'What is it regarding, Mr Hardy?'

Quick study. 'Arson,' I said. 'Possibly.'

He nodded and picked up the phone. 'Door on your right. Down the passage. First left.'

I went as directed. The building had been worked on over the years to provide private offices. I knocked at the door with 'Detectives' stencilled on it, got the call and went in. Biggish room, big windows, skylight, three desks each with a computer, filing cabinets, shelves stuffed with paper, photocopier, wastepaper baskets spewing. The carpet was dirty, likewise the windows. That didn't mean anything— my office carpet hadn't been too clean and the windows were opaque unless there'd been heavy rain. There were two men at their desks. The one who looked up was beefy and balding with a bull neck. Had to be Barton. I wondered if his first name was Bruce.

He beckoned me over. 'Let's have a look at the credentials.'

I handed him the folder, pulled up a chair and sat down without being asked. He didn't like it. He didn't like my licence folder or anything about me. He dropped the folder on the desk where I'd have to stretch to retrieve it. I didn't.

'To what d'we owe the honour?'

'Oh, I'm just letting you know I'm around. In case anything happens. You know.'

'Smartarse. Specifically?'

He sat very still, didn't fidget and kept his eyes focused on my face. I got a sense that, while he might have been rigid and narrow-minded, he wasn't incompetent.

'I'm working for Dr Elizabeth Farmer.'

'Oh, yeah? Doing what?'

'Enquiring into her father's death.'

He smiled, showing expensively capped teeth. He liked showing them. He'd had good advice about his hair; it was on the retreat but it was dark, clipped closely and didn't look sad. I noticed that his shirt wasn't from the bargain bin, nor his tie. His suit jacket was draped on a wooden hanger from a stand behind him. Hung smoothly.

'On a daily rate, are you? Expenses and all? That'd be a nice money-spinner. Good luck.'

'Nothing else to say, Sergeant? No doubts?'

'There's always doubts. I've got more than a few about you.'

I took my notebook out and flipped it open. 'A witness reported a suspicious person on site before the fire.'

'So you didn't check in first before you started snooping around?'

'Checking in's the second thing I did.'

For the first time he shifted his considerable weight in his chair. He was either bored or good at seeming to be. 'Unreliable information. Vague, unsubstantiated.'

'So much information is, until it's investigated and . . . put together with other things.'

His colleague, who'd seemed to be concentrating on his paperwork, shot a look across at us, but dropped his head again immediately.

'You're wasting your time and your client's money, Hardy,' Barton said.

He pushed the folder across to me. I stood up and collected it.

'Thank you for *your* time,' I said.

'Not a problem. Make sure your vehicle's roadworthy.'

I drove into Wollongong and located the offices of the Illawarra Mutual Insurance Company. I was told that Mr Lucas was out of the office. I got his mobile number and rang him. The background noise was unmistakable— Mr Lucas was in the pub. I told him I was a private investigator and his enthusiasm almost welled out of the phone. Meet me? He'd buy me a drink, several drinks.

The hotel was down near the railway station. It was old-fashioned with the stylised beer advertisements showing flappers and men in flannels still in place, though badly faded. You could almost see the ghosts of the weary travellers who'd trudged up the steps from the sunken station to find comfort there. For the time of day there was good activity in the bar of the old kind—drinking and yarning—rather than the new sort—pool and pokies. Lucas had described himself as stunningly handsome with a body like a Greek god. I said I was middle-aged, tall, greying and with a broken nose.

I took a few steps inside and a small, slight young man with gelled fair hair wearing a dark suit that was a bit too big for him hopped off his bar stool and came towards me. He had a schooner of beer in his left hand. He extended the right.

'You'd be Hardy.'

I shook his hand. A firm, dry grip, stronger than I'd expected from someone his size. 'I would,' I said.

'Good to meet you. Come and have a drink. Had lunch?'

I shook my head.

'They do a great steak sandwich here. I've ordered. Want one?'

'Sure.'

We reached the bar and he signalled with two fingers to the woman working at the counter-lunch section. She nodded and forced a smile.

'What'll you have?'

The orange juice and coffee at the motel and the coffee at Sue Holland's place were a distant memory. Since then I'd swum, been given the cold shoulder and driven a bit. I hadn't spent much of Elizabeth Farmer's money yet. 'Middy of old,' I said.

He was about to signal to the barman but I reached over, put a five dollar note on the bar, and gave my order.

Lucas sighed and took a pull on his beer. 'Like that,' he said. 'Okay.'

'I'll let you buy the lunch,' I said. 'Where can we talk?'

We went through to a saloon bar where the food was served. Using one hand, Lucas deftly gathered up napkins and cutlery and dumped the lot on a table. He went back for salt and pepper and hot sauce. I sat down and worked on my drink.

Lucas patted his pockets and then shook his head. 'I forgot. Can't smoke in here now. Probably better. What d'you want to talk about . . .' he glanced down at the card I'd put on the table, '. . . Cliff?'

'A fire insurance claim you investigated, allegedly.'

He lowered the level in his glass substantially. 'Are you trying to piss me off?'

'No. I'm just letting you know there are questions to be asked.'

'Aren't there always. I—'

'I was in your game for a while,' I said. 'Quite a few back, but in a small firm, like yours. I know how things work.'

'Okay. Name of claimant?'

'Farmer.'

'Oh, Jesus.' He expelled a long breath and looked down at his almost empty glass. High heels clacked on the floor. 'Good, here's the tucker.'

I let him have his moment of respite as the woman expertly slid the plates onto the table. Two toasted slices of grainy bread with thick slabs of meat between them, surrounded by a mass of lettuce and slices of tomato and beetroot with piles of chips taking up the rest of the space on the plate. A very honest serve.

'Complimentary glasses of wine, sirs?' the woman said. She was in her thirties and looked tired, but she was close to chic in her tight black dress, cropped hair and heels.

I nodded. 'Red, thanks.'

Lucas emptied his schooner in a short gulp and handed it to her, 'Thanks, Maggie. Same for me.'

I picked up a perfectly crisp chip. 'Most days, this'd do me for lunch and dinner.'

'It does me,' Lucas said.

The glasses of red wine came and it was out of a bottle, not a cask. We ate for a while and then I forced him to meet my eye.

'Come on,' I said.

He shrugged. 'Well, you say you know how it goes.

Some claims you get the word to go full bottle on and some you don't.'

'That was the case with the Farmer claim?'

'Yep. It's nothing obvious. Just how quickly the paperwork gets to you, how clear it is that everything's kosher administratively. A hint that quick clearances are desirable this month.'

I thought that over while I ate. The meal was good and I was enjoying it. Lucas didn't look as comfortable. He dribbled hot sauce on his food.

'So why?' I said.

'I'd be speculating.'

'Speculate.'

'What's in it for me?'

'A clear conscience.'

He laughed. 'You watch *Yes, Minister*?'

'Sure.'

'Sir Humphrey says a clear conscience is a luxury.'

'Two hundred, two fifty—depending on the quality of the speculation.'

He took a mouthful and chewed deliberately, swallowed. 'That as high as you can go?'

'I'm being generous. I can speculate myself.'

'Usually,' he said slowly, 'this kind of . . . understanding results when a party that puts a large amount of business an insurance company's way has an interest in the outcome of the claim in question.'

'Couldn't have put it better myself,' I said.

7

That was all I could get out of him on the subject. If Carson Lucas knew or suspected which clients of Illawarra Insurance had an interest in the Farmer claim he wasn't going to tell me and there was no way I could make him. Not that I could think of at the time. I'd certainly give it more thought. A developer of some sort seemed most likely given what Sue Holland had told me, but developers come in all shapes and sizes and their company names don't always give a clue as to what they are or do.

'Cunt of a job, this,' Lucas said as he finished his food.

'Investigating insurance? Better than selling it.'

'I dunno.'

'Work on commission, don't they? No sale, no dough. That's a point. Who sold Frederick Farmer his insurance?'

Lucas found a last chip or two among the lettuce he wasn't intending to eat. 'Bloke called Adam MacPherson. Used to drink here. Haven't seen him for a while.'

'Is he still with the company?'

'How about my two-fifty?'

We went to an ATM near the bank of pokies and I drew out the money.

'MacPherson?'

'The answer is no.' Lucas plucked the notes from my hand and strode away.

I went to the toilet and freshened up. Then I went back into the lounge and ordered a cup of coffee. The waitress in the black who'd served the food and drink worked the machine like an expert and I told her so.

'Should be. I've been here long enough.'

'Ah, Maggie, did that bloke I was with give you a tip?' I asked.

'Never does.'

I paid for the coffee with a twenty-dollar note. 'You can keep the change as a tip and for a bit of information.'

She shot a look to right and left before taking the money. A lifted eyebrow indicated agreement.

'Adam MacPherson. Drinks in here, I'm told. Do you know him?'

'Yeah, he's a regular. Not in the daytime, but.'

'So he's in, what? Most nights?'

'Yeah.'

'Last question—what's he look like?'

She wasn't dumb. 'Who are you, then?'

I showed her my licence and gave her a card. 'This is nothing heavy. I just want to ask him a few questions.' I grinned. 'I'm big on questions. Might be worth money to him.'

'He could use it.' She described MacPherson to me, slid the coffee across and slipped away. Not a bad morning's work, I thought. Good coffee, too.

. . .

I walked back to the car park where I'd left the Falcon and called Elizabeth Farmer on my mobile.

'Dr Farmer, this is Cliff Hardy. I'm in Wollongong.'

'Good,' she said. 'Are you making any progress?'

'Possibly. I met your neighbour, Sue Holland. She told me she saw someone mysterious around the house before your father died. I'm wondering why you didn't tell me about that.'

'Because I didn't know.'

'Ms Holland didn't tell you? I had the impression you were friends.'

'*Were* friends. Not for some time. Is this necessary? If that information is accurate I expect you'll follow up on it.'

I thought I got the picture. 'Okay. A few more things. Am I right in thinking the insurance claim was settled quickly?'

'Do you mean on the property or Dad's life?'

'The property.'

'Yes, quite quickly. I know because that involved me. I don't know about the life insurance. You'd have to ask Matilda. She was the beneficiary.'

'Okay. Last thing. Have you had any offers to buy the Wombarra block?'

'Yes.'

'Who from?'

'From whom. Sorry, I'm being a shit. I just feel a bit besieged by all these questions. I could've filled you in on all this beforehand if I'd known.'

'I understand, but the questions come up as things move along. And that's the last one. From whom?'

She laughed. 'Fair enough. From Matilda, who else?

And before you have to ask another question, I can tell you I told her to go fuck herself.'

'Thank you, Dr Farmer. I'll be in touch.'

It was one of those situations. Could Lucas be trusted to keep my interest in the Farmer matter to himself? Could Sergeant Barton be trusted? Lucas, maybe, because I'd given him money. Barton, only if he was honest. If either or both of them had agendas of their own I could be in for some trouble. Nothing new.

I pulled out of the car park and drove to where I do my best thinking—the beach. Wollongong City Beach had a long sweep south of Flagstaff Point. The shoreline had been modified by an extensive breakwater, a common feature on the Illawarra coast, where the sea resists human activity. I parked opposite some up-market apartment blocks and sat in a small park that boasted some old guns that predated the artificial harbour where classy yachts rode at anchor. At a guess, the guns had been placed in the 1890s to repel a Russian attack that never came. Along the street I found an undamaged telephone directory at the bus shelter. How many A. MacPhersons could there be in the area? As it turned out, none. Worth a try.

The day had warmed up considerably and I shed my jacket and walked along the beach. The sky was cloudy and the water was greyish-looking. Not a picture postcard vista, but still, for an industrial city, not a bad stretch of sand and water. I could see boats heading in and out of the harbour, yachts and fishing boats. The freight activity would be further south at Port Kembla and there were container ships on the horizon.

I reached an outcrop of rocks and squatted. I was having trouble concentrating on the Farmer business. Something about this beach and seascape was getting to me, drawing me. Wollongong was a city with a history—union struggles, political battles, environmental issues and plenty of crime. I dimly recalled cases involving a predatory rapist, a headless corpse and, more recently, revenge killings of alleged paedophiles. It wasn't everybody's set of positives, but for a man in my line of work . . .

My mobile broke into this reverie.

'Hardy.'

'This is Phil at Silken Touch. Kristina's phoned. Says she's coming in tonight.'

'Shit.'

'What's wrong? I thought you wanted to see her.'

'Yeah. Right. What time'll she be there?'

'With these bitches who can say? Eleven, midnight?'

'I'll be there.'

He rang off. Suddenly, working two cases at once didn't seem like such a good idea. I could get back to Sydney in an hour and a half, more or less, depending on the traffic. That meant I'd have to leave the 'Gong at nine-thirty at the latest. Would MacPherson show up at the pub by that time? Would he show up at all? I had hours to kill before following up on something that was by no means a certainty. One of those times when an assistant would have come in handy. I had one of a sort in Hank Bachelor, who was on a small retainer to provide backup from time to time. But this wasn't the sort of thing I could hand over to him.

I got up and stretched, feeling less flexible than I liked to feel. A legacy of neglect of the gym and accumulated birthdays. I mooched along the sand, kicking at plastic bottles and bits of driftwood brought in by the tide. A rogue wave rose abruptly and washed over my feet and I swore. Suddenly, I was much less enamoured of the Illawarra. Sydney was my go, along with the pollution and the traffic, aggro from the likes of Harry and the phoney glamour of places like The Silken Touch. I realised I was veering towards self-pity and shook the feeling off. I left the beach, found a park bench, took off my shoes and wrung out my socks. A passer-by smiled at me and I smiled back.

At 7 pm, back wearing my jeans, sneakers, T-shirt and a denim jacket that lives mustily in the car, I was in the bar of the pub nursing a schooner of light. Maggie had described MacPherson in detail—stocky, fortyish, red hair and beard, a smoker and Guinness drinker. Loner. I stayed in the bar where smoking was permitted, at least for now, ate some crisps, played the pokies without concentration or luck, tried to show some interest in the soccer on TV. Hard to do. I went through the saloon bar to the toilet and saw that Maggie was on duty.

'You work a long day,' I said.

'I've got ends to make meet,' she said. 'No sign of your bloke so far, eh?'

'No.' I looked at my watch. 'I can't give him much longer. Have to get back to Sydney.'

'Wish I could come with you. But my husband and two kids might object.'

I laughed. 'Well, I'll be back.'

She mimed shock. 'You keep away from me. If he doesn't show before you leave and comes in later, d'you want me to give him a message?'

I thought about it. 'Why not?' I gave her my card and ten dollars. 'Tell him to give me a ring.'

'Ooh, a private eye. Maybe I will come to Sydney with you.'

'It's not all it's cracked up to be.'

'Your glass is empty. You've paid for another one. What'll it be?'

'Middy of light.'

'That's right. You're driving.'

She gave me the drink and went about her work. Back in the smoky bar, where the noise level from the pokies, the drunks and the pool players was rising, I looked around for the stocky redhead with no luck. I left the pub and reached my car with only ninety minutes to get to Alexandria. I was only a couple of blocks away when I saw the flashing blue light in the rear vision. The police car drew alongside and I pulled over.

Two uniforms. Both youngish. One stayed in the car, the other fronted, gestured for me to lower the window.

'I believe you just left the hotel, sir.'

'That's right.'

He produced the bag with the mouthpiece. 'Blow into the tube, please.'

I knew what was happening. Barton had put the word out. I'd had twenty-five ounces of light beer over a three hour period. Safe enough, but maybe not with nothing to eat except a packet of crisps. How light is light? How much soak-up is there in crisps? I accepted the device and blew.

He examined the crystals. 'Okay,' he said. 'Just. Drive carefully, Mr Hardy.'

. . .

Things were very different at the brothel when I got there a
little after eleven. Quite a few cars were parked nearby and,
instead of letting me in, the gate remained closed and the
receptionist said Phil would be out to see me. As he came
out a taxi pulled up and a woman got out. Not Kristina.
She was at least 185 centimetres tall in her heels and her
hair added a bit to that. The elegantly tailored coat opened
to reveal a generous figure in a tight red dress. A silk scarf
did the job of concealing the Adam's apple but the breadth
of shoulder was a giveaway. She gave me a winning lip gloss
and mascara smile.

'Shy, darling?' A hand with scarlet fingernails touched
my sleeve.

'I'm waiting for Phil.'

She came closer, still smiling, and the hand moved to
my crotch. 'Wasting your time, sweetheart. He's straight.
I, on the other hand . . .'

'Evening, Roberta,' Phil said from behind the gate.
'Don't bother the man. He's here on business.'

Roberta pursed her lips and pecked me on the cheek.
She shrugged; her breasts bounced and the gate swung
open. She went in and Phil came out. He was in his night-
time work clothes—Italian suit, blue shirt, dark tie. He
drew in a deep breath as if he needed fresh air and then
fished out cigarettes and lit one. He offered me the packet
and I shook my head.

'Would you believe? It's a no-smoking knocking-shop.'

'Is she here?'

'Not yet. I wanted to get a few things straight.'

Roberta's scent hung heavily in the air. 'Like what?'

He blew a plume of smoke. 'I asked around about you,
Hardy. You come up okay. A man of your word, sort of.'

'Glad to hear it.'

'Just thought I'd tell you I've got some insurance. Tape of you giving me money, you with Roberta . . . See what I mean?'

'Clever,' I said.

'Careful. When this cunt arrives you take her away and do whatever you like, but she was never here. Understand?'

What I understood was how good he was at what he did. From the way he stood, balanced and steady, I could tell that the cigarette could be flicked in my face in an instant if required, and the blow would be a nanosecond behind.

'I understand,' I said. 'What you have to understand is that I'm likely to be back when my business with Kristina is all over.'

'Look forward to it. She should be here any minute.' He'd only taken one drag on the cigarette. It hadn't been for smoking. He dropped it, pressed the buzzer and went through the gate.

I went back to my car and waited. Fifteen minutes later a taxi drew up and a young woman got out. She wore white trousers, white high heels and a white leather coat. There was a white band in her hair. She paid the driver and tripped across to the gate. She buzzed and leaned close to hear the intercom. She straightened up, hitched up her white shoulder bag and looked ready to break something, anything.

'Kristina,' I spoke quietly and approached in as non-threatening a manner as I could.

Anger had brought a flush to her face. Phil had been right. She looked much older than her years, but the white outfit lent her a kind of vulnerability, no doubt deliberately contrived. 'Who the fuck are you? What do you want?'

'I'm a private detective. Your mother hired me to find you. She's worried about you. With good reason I'd say.'

'Fuck off.'

'If I do, what d'you do next? I've had a word here. You're out.'

'There's plenty of places.'

I shook my head. 'Not for you. Not with me along telling them how old you are.'

'Fuck you.'

'You should've stayed at school. You need a wider vocabulary. So what d' you reckon? I can't see you in William Street, doing it in the backs of cars.'

'You say *she* hired you?'

'That's right.'

'Can't be paying much.' She opened her coat. She wore a tight, low-dipping white lacy top. No bra. Her nipples poked through the lace. 'Maybe we could come to a different arrangement.'

'I don't think so.'

'Man of steel. Well . . .'

A car drew up. 'Let's continue this a bit further away. I don't think Phil'd like us blocking up the access.'

She said, 'You scared of Phil?' but she moved with me away towards my car.

'Under the right conditions, no. Under the wrong ones, yes.'

It's a technique—keep 'em talking, keep 'em moving.

'What would the right conditions be, then?'

'Probably him drunk and me with a shotgun.'

Kristina laughed, still moving. A nice, musical laugh. Very commercial.

'We're out of the same box, Phil and me, ex-army, but he's got youth on his side.'

'You're not so old.'

We were almost to my car. 'Knock it off, Krissy,' I said. 'I—'

She burst into tears. 'Don't call me that. I'm not Krissy.'

'I was just trying . . .'

She sagged against the car and suddenly looked her age, or close to it. Her heavy eye makeup had run and in brushing at her mouth she'd spread her lipstick up her cheek. The arriving client took a quick look at us, checked his stride but then continued on. Not a good Samaritan tonight.

She sniffed, rummaged in her bag for a tissue and cleaned up. 'I might as well go and see her,' she said. 'See what's on her mind.'

I nodded. 'I'll drive you.'

She gave me a fierce stare. 'I'm not saying I'm going to stay!'

I shrugged. 'Between you and her.' I unlocked the passenger door. 'Get in.'

I got in and started up. 'Put your belt on.'

'Yes, Daddy.'

'Knock it off. And do up your coat.'

She pushed out her chest. 'Don't you like them?'

I didn't answer and got moving. She closed her coat, buckled on her belt and sulked.

8

'I can't go home like this,' Kristina Karatsky said. She waved her hand at her outfit. 'You have to take me to my place to change.'

'Okay. Where would that be?'

'Paddo.' She gave me the street and the number.

'Bit of a jump up from Tempe.'

'I was slumming.'

Puzzling. Somehow she didn't seem like the runaway I'd been expecting from her mother's description, the photograph, the T-shirt, the Tempe housemates. Her clothes were expensive. The multiple earrings and the nose-ring were gone. She wore elegant, stylish earrings. Her makeup, before she smudged it, had been perfect and a quick glance showed me that her nails were manicured and perfectly painted.

'What're you looking at?'

'I'm wondering how you got to be this flash so quickly.'

'You think I'm flash?'

'Don't start. You know what I mean.'

She shrugged, reached into her bag and took out cigarettes.

'No,' I said.

'Fuckin' puritan.'

'Light that and I'll take it and burn a hole in your coat.'

She sighed, dropped the packet back in the bag and stroked the leather. 'Know what this cost?'

'No. Do you?'

'Have you got a woman?'

I didn't answer.

'Probably not, from the look of you. Or some daggy droob in a tracker and flatties.'

I did the rest of the drive in silence. She stared out the window at the cars and the lights and the people as if they had nothing to do with her. I wound through the Paddington streets and pulled up outside a smart terrace—three storeys, white, black wrought iron, crafted front garden. 'Are you sure this's you?'

She did a quick repair job on her face, opened the door and stepped out. 'Surprised, aren't you? Come on, but give me some space. Not quite sure who'll be home.'

I stayed a little ahead and opened the gate. She glided past, brushing against me, and I wondered if she was going to start playing games again. We went up the steps and she rang the bell. I waited a metre away. Footsteps sounded and the door opened. She was as quick as Cathy Freeman. The coat was open, the tits were showing and she was screaming as she pushed me away.

'Help me, help me. He's hurting me.'

The guy who came through the door was big with muscles bulging inside a too-tight T-shirt. He was also very fired up. Kristina ducked away and he was on me before I could react. I just managed to stop his punch from landing squarely but the weight of it, catching my shoulder, rocked me and I hit the wall. My head bounced off the bricks and I went down with noises booming inside my skull. That little bit of the world spun and kept spinning. I felt cold bricks behind and cold tiles underneath me, and I knew I had to close my eyes in order to take a breath—couldn't do both at the same time.

When I decided I could breathe and open my eyes without everything echoing and spinning, I found the man who had hit me standing over me and sounding apologetic. Couldn't be true. I closed my eyes again.

'Jesus, mate, I'm sorry. Are you all right?'

'What?'

'She was bullshitting. She took off.'

'Took off, where, how?'

'Fuck, she just ran down the steps through the gate and jumped into this old heap outside and took off.'

Although it hurt and I knew it wasn't going to do any good, I felt in the pocket of my jacket for the keys.

'She took my car,' I said. 'She doesn't live here?'

He shook his head and, with my vision clearing, I had a closer look at him. Thirtyish, balding, built like a bull. I felt I should know his name but couldn't bring it up. Almost, but not quite. For such a formidable figure he suddenly looked embarrassed, sheepish, vulnerable. I eased myself up, sliding against the brickwork, until I was at eye level with him. I turned my head to the open gate and the blank space in front of the house.

'You assaulted me. She stole my car.'

'Jesus, mate . . .'

Another vocabulary-poor individual, although the other one had had tricks up her sleeve. She knew this address and the resident. The picture was becoming clearer. 'We'd better have a talk,' I said. I took my wallet out and showed him the licence. 'A place like this'd have a couple of bathrooms, right? And, Jason, a bloke like you'd have something on hand to drink.'

The name had come to me in a flash—Jason Garvan was an almost legendary rugby player. A fan of the Ellas in the past, I'd followed rugby in spurts and it was hard to open a paper a few years back without seeing his picture. He switched from League after a dispute in the club and then came into the big money when rugby went professional. Not so prominent now. He didn't look happy that I'd recognised him, but he was smart enough to know he had to play along with me.

We went into the house, which was done up in the way a professional decorator treats an inner-city terrace. They start out looking like mine when the yuppies buy them and they end up looking like this—painted, carpeted, polished. The front room off the passage served as a kind of den-cum-bar-cum-memorabilia room. Trophies galore in a couple of cabinets, photographs showing Jason with celebrities and team photographs on the walls.

He went behind the bar. 'What'll it be?'

'Brandy.' I sank into a chair and felt the back of my head. My hair was matted with blood but the wound had stopped seeping. Better not to lean back against his leather upholstery just the same. He gave me a tumbler half full of brandy and poured a solid vodka for himself. I took a swig. Smooth.

'Thanks,' I said. 'Don't worry, I'm not going to make trouble for you, although God knows I could.'

'You'll have to report your car stolen, but.'

'Could've happened anywhere. I'm talking about you having sex with an underage female and assaulting me.'

'Jesus, mate . . .'

'If you say that again I'll change my mind. Just shut up and let me sit here for a bit and think.'

He wasn't used to men he outmeasured and outweighed telling him what to do, but he squatted on a stool, sipped his drink and watched me. After a while he asked me what I was working on. I told him and it didn't make him any happier. Quite the opposite—he poured another drink.

'That's not going to do your speed any good.'

He was about to tell me to get fucked but thought better of it. I drank half the brandy and felt steadier but the headache was building.

'Got any painkillers?'

Of course he did. He nodded and left the room. The mobile in my jacket pocket rang. I answered and Kristina's voice came through clear and crisp.

'Your crappy car's in Oxford Street near the barracks. The keys'll be under the front seat. I hope you're not too badly hurt. Leave me fucking-well alone.'

I put the phone back in my pocket, downed the rest of the brandy and grabbed the bottle from the bar. I walked out leaving the front door open. Give Jason something to think about apart from tackles and knock-ons.

Every step I took along the streets of Paddington sent shock waves through me and I wished I'd stayed for the painkillers. I found the car exactly where she said it'd be and sat in the seat quietly for a minute to make sure I was up to the drive. My bag was there, untouched, also the books and other bits and pieces. A card with my mobile number on it was crumpled up on the seat. The keys were under the seat.

I stopped at the first open chemist, bought painkillers and washed them down with a paper cup of water while the pharmacist looked shocked at the number I took.

'You'll shred your liver,' he said.

Oncoming lights dazzled me, rough patches on the road shook me and the analgesics on top of the hefty dose of brandy made me light-headed. I drove, gritting my teeth and forcing myself to focus on every movement. I thought if I allowed myself to drift into auto-pilot mode I could finish up in Parramatta or wrapped around a lamppost. If the cops found me in this condition, with the open bottle of brandy in the car, I'd be off the road for six months.

No maudlin thoughts about not wanting to go home this time. My door, my hall, my kitchen, my bathroom had never looked so good. I stripped, had a shower and cleaned the head wound with alcohol swabs. I hadn't eaten since the pub lunch, so I slapped together some leftovers and microwaved the lot into a sort of bubble-and-squeak. I ate a few mouthfuls and then threw the lot up into the sink. I knew I was slightly concussed and couldn't remember the treatment. I filled a plastic bag with ice cubes and held it to my head. Better.

I sat in the living room wrapped in a towelling robe, holding the plastic bag to my head. Some detective. I'd caught my quarry and let her get away by completely mis-reading her. Something had happened to Kristina between Tempe and when I'd met her. That sounded right—at least I was thinking again. Where had the clothes and accessories come from? She couldn't have gone far even in Paddington at that time of night, dressed as she was, without courting trouble, so how had she been able to ditch the car so soon? She could have ducked in somewhere and called a cab on her mobile. Maybe. But where was she going? On balance it looked to me as if she had a provider, a protector. A pimp.

I went upstairs to bed wondering how I was going to communicate this to her mother. I crawled in, still wearing the robe. My last thought was that I'd been propositioned three times in the course of the day. Two had been commercial and the other was only in fun.

9

I phoned Marisha Karatsky and said I had news of her daughter although I hadn't exactly located her.

'You've seen her? Spoken to her?'

'Yes.'

'She's well . . . not sick?'

'No, but I have to talk to you.'

She worked from her home in Dulwich Hill. The building had been a large warehouse now divided into apartments. Security door. I buzzed the number she'd given me. She had a top level spot—large floor space, open plan kitchen and living and three bedrooms. Pricey, depending on when she bought it. Maybe she rented. Expensive either way. She invited me in and brewed up some coffee. She wore a long smock over black flared trousers. As a rule small people shouldn't wear flared pants, but she managed to look good. The heels helped. We sat at a low table with the coffee mugs. A large window gave a wide view of nothing in particular. It let in a lot of light and my head still ached. She saw me wince.

'What's the matter?'

'I got hit on the head. The light bothers me a bit.'

She drew some curtains and everything softened. 'Not by Kristina, I hope.'

'No. By a brick wall. Although she helped.'

'Oh, my God. I'm sorry.'

'It's all right. Goes with the job. Nothing serious.'

I told her everything from Tempe to Paddington via Alexandria without pulling any punches. She sipped her coffee and her face remained expressionless although her dark eyes with the shadows beneath them seemed to become more hooded. My coffee was cool by the time I finished but I drank it anyway, along with a couple of painkillers from the supply in my pocket.

'Fifteen,' she said, 'and a whore.'

'For what it's worth,' I said. 'It could be worse. The Alexandria place is well run. She seems to be able to look after herself. The guy there said she tested clear for drugs. I'm inclined to believe him.'

'But at the house in Tempe they said—'

'Could've been a pose. I'm not saying she's not a very confused and conflicted young woman.'

She stood and began to pace around the big room, her high heels clacking on the polished floorboards. Watching her, I began to see similarities between her and her daughter despite the difference in size—the same mass of dark hair, facial refinement, grace of movement. She sat down and leaned towards me across the table, her eyes huge, her mouth trembling.

'I wasn't entirely honest with you, Mr Hardy.'

I tried a reassuring grin. 'Like the knock on the head, it goes with the job.'

'You say her clothes . . . the white clothes looked expensive?'

'Very.'

She said, 'Shit,' pronouncing it almost like a foreign word. 'I thought when I found the Tempe address and from the clothes she was wearing lately she was at least being . . . you saw the T-shirt—a pinball place.'

I nodded.

'I thought you might find her working at a fast food place, smoking dope, taking ecstasy at dance parties. Bad enough, but not . . .'

She was shaking, coming apart. I moved around the table to the two-seater chair and put my arm around her shoulders. She drew closer, her small body seeming to shrink into my bulk.

'What, Marisha?'

'Not with . . . him.'

'Who?'

She didn't move away and she stopped shaking after a while. It was some time since I'd been that close to a woman and I enjoyed the contact. Her hair smelled of herbal shampoo and I wanted to stroke it.

'I . . . there was a man. I was with him for a time. I thought he was a good man but one day I found him with Kristina. He had bought her clothes and makeup and shoes and she was all dressed up for him. I don't think he had . . . what's the word?'

'Molested?'

'Yes, molested. I don't think so, but I wasn't sure. Perhaps it was not the first time. I sent him away and I threw out the things. Kristina screamed. A big fight, but she calmed down.'

'When was this?'

She pulled away then and I let her go. She turned her

head to look up at me and there were questions as well as pain in her eyes. Something had happened between us, and it wasn't to do with Kristina. The reaction I'd had to her at my place was back, stronger.

'Two years ago. She was thirteen. She was always precocious . . .'

'No,' I gripped her wrist. 'That's wrong. With a kid of thirteen, the responsibility is always on the adult. Always, Marisha!'

'Yes. You are right. He telephoned and I know she spoke to him again. I changed the number. We moved to this place. She saw a counsellor for a little time and I thought . . .'

'Did he have money, this guy?'

'Yes, he had money. I think so.'

'You think so.' I couldn't help a critical note creeping in. 'How long were you with him?'

She pulled right away and leaned back. A long breath, in and out. 'It is difficult to explain, Mr Hardy.'

'Cliff—my name's Cliff.'

'Cliff. You said you had a daughter you hadn't raised— perhaps you will understand.'

I was willing. I eased away and nodded.

'I came to this country twelve years ago. Kristina's father had died, but his brother was here and he . . . sponsored me and my daughter. I had university degrees from Poland but they weren't recognised. I had to study to get qualifications and to improve my English. I worked—cleaning, kitchens in restaurants, waitressing—it was very hard. But slowly I improved. I could speak English. An educated person in Poland speaks English.'

'They teach languages better there than we do here,' I said. 'I can barely read a French menu.'

'But I wanted to work with words, with language. Words are my passion, my . . .'

'Talent,' I said. 'I can see that.'

She smiled. 'Thank you. I got the Australian degree and I began to get translating work with different companies—leaflets, websites . . .'

'You picked that up too?'

'I did. It's not so hard. What's wrong?'

'Not a thing. I'm impressed.'

'I don't understand that. I still have difficulties. But with all this work I neglected her, Kristina. I tried, but I failed. She began not going to school, missing . . . ?'

'Wagging, we used to say. Then it was jigging, now I think it's ditching.'

'English is such a strange language. Yes. I was worried. Then I met Stefan, Steve as he called himself. Swedish, handsome. He said he had heard I had a number of languages and he wanted something translated from Swedish. I know Polish, German, French and Russian. Not much Swedish, but . . .' Her elegant shrug filled in the gap.

'This is him?'

'Yes. Stefan Parnevik. I'm still not sure what he did for money, but he had a lot. A car, clothes, credit cards. All these were things I wanted and would work to get, but they were still not there yet for me. He gave me money. Enough to put a deposit on a little flat. He was there often. He took me to dinner. I . . . felt stronger. I had more time. I got more work at better pay. I paid off as much of the mortgage as I could, very fast. Then I found Stefan and Kristina together in the way I said.'

Telling the story was exhausting her and I told her to stop. There was still coffee in the pot and I took the cups and microwaved it. A Hardy special, never mind if it makes it bitter—good excuse for sugar.

She'd composed herself when I got back with the coffee and the haunted look had receded a bit. 'I didn't think I'd ever have to talk about this,' she said.

'You say there were phone calls after you kicked him out. Was there any face-to-face contact?'

She shook her head. 'With me, no. I thought he was ashamed, perhaps fearful of what I would do. I did nothing, partly . . . partly because I didn't want to make it too big for Kristina. She said nothing happened. Perhaps I was wrong to . . .'

'Hard to say. Do you think he saw her, met her?'

'I don't know. After a time she calmed down and began to seem normal. But normal for Kristina was not normal as for other girls. Oh God, what am I going to do?'

'Find her. And give him to the police. If this is all the way we think it is, he's connived at having an underage girl work as a prostitute. And it's more than likely that he . . .'

'Yes.'

'So where is he? Where does he live?'

She'd taken a decent swig of the coffee as if to prepare herself for something. And here it was. 'I don't know,' she said.

'What?'

'Don't say it like that, Cliff, please. I never went to his place; he always came to mine. I didn't ask any questions. I was looking, hoping for someone and he was . . . charismatic.'

'Charismatic.'

'Yes. Yes. Good-looking, kind, generous. And funny.'

'Funny'll do it.'

'Do it?'

I knew what I meant—funny is hard to compete with—but I didn't want to lay it out for her because I knew I'd sound jealous however I put it and she'd know. 'Well, finding people is my speciality, so I guess I'll just have to set about it.'

She took in more coffee and didn't say anything. I felt wrong-footed and fidgeted with the coffee mug, waiting for her to speak. When she didn't I moved back close, put my hand to her face and turned it towards me. Her skin was soft against my hard, gym and tennis-calloused palm.

'Marisha, I want to help you.'

'You despise me.'

'I don't.'

'You despise me for letting my daughter fall into the hands of such a man.'

'No.' I had one hand on her cheek and the other on her shoulder and I drew her towards me. I bent and she strained upwards. Her eyes were wide and her mouth was opening. I felt I had to stop her speaking, saying no. I kissed her and she returned the kiss fiercely and gripped me with a strength I wouldn't have thought possible. The kiss lasted so long I was struggling for breath when it ended. I realised we were both panting and we reached for each other again, colliding rather than embracing.

Her bedroom was dim and smelled of incense. The bed smelled of her. She eased herself off from where she'd straddled me and rolled to one side. I put out my arm and she shaped her small body to mine, clinging close.

'Was it wrong?' she said.

'Didn't feel wrong to me. Felt very right.'

'No, I know it's not like a doctor and patient. I meant with Kristina . . .'

I loved her smell—the combination of shampoo and perfume and her body. I inhaled, buried my face in her hair, kissed her ear. 'I read that in the London Blitz, in the war,' I said, 'people made love where they were sheltering, in cellars, the tube stations, with other people around. Some-times with strangers. Stress broke down barriers. That's really something, given that we're talking about the English.'

'You say *the English* like that, but you're English, surely?'

'Only half on one side—the rest's a mixture of Irish and French and God knows what. My maternal grandmother was a gypsy. She'd have said you had gypsy eyes.' I ran a finger lightly across the dark skin under her eyes.

'No, no. No Romany that I know of. But in Europe, who knows? Jewish certainly, on one side as you say. Cliff, you think this is just . . . stress?'

'No,' I said. 'I don't think so.' And I meant it, although the speed of our coming together like that was a little surprising. But the times are strange and everything's speeded up.

10

I spent the rest of the morning with Marisha Karatsky, interestedly if not productively. I inspected the room that had been Kristina's. Marisha had said she'd shown me everything useful on our first meeting, but parents only ever know part of their kids' stories. The quick look I had confirmed my impression—that the girl I'd been looking for hardly bore any resemblance to the young woman I'd found, and lost. Except for one thing. Kristina had had a hiding place—a gap between the skirting board and the wall. It was only wide enough to contain a few small things—a couple of joints maybe, money, condoms. I probed it with my Swiss army knife and came up with a five dollar note and a card. The card had a name scrawled on it, Karen Bach, and an address. No phone number.

Marisha's work room was a mass of books, keyboards, screens, tape recorders and other machines I couldn't identify.

'Everything is digital now,' she said. 'Or will be soon.'

'So they tell me. I'm barely analogue, myself.'

She laughed. We drank more coffee and made love again.

'I only had two condoms,' she said afterwards.

'Just as well. Twice in eight hours is my total limit. Plus I have to go to work.'

My mobile rang in the pocket of my jacket, lying on a chair under her smock. As I bent to find it I realised that I hadn't been aware of my head hurting for hours.

'Hardy.'

'Mr Hardy, this is Detective Sergeant Aronson at Glebe. I believe we've met.'

Aronson. I tried to place him, put him in context. A case about a year ago when my investigation of an attempted murder and suicide had crossed with that of the police. We'd remained mutually civil, just. 'Yes, Sergeant.'

'I'd like you to come to the station as soon as possible, please.'

Marisha was looking enquiringly at me by this time. I tried to mime business, but probably didn't succeed. She shrugged and went away.

'About what?'

'I'd rather tell you when you get here.'

'And I'd rather you told me now or at least gave me a hint. Otherwise, I'm on to my lawyer and we talk about it.'

'Feeling threatened, Hardy?'

I noted the dropped mister and wasn't surprised. Police courtesy to people in my trade is always skin deep.

'It's to do with one Adam Ian MacPherson.'

It seemed a long time ago and a lot had happened since, so my confused response was genuine. 'I'm not sure—'

'Come on, Hardy. You were asking about him in a Wollongong pub last night. He was found shot dead in Fairy Meadow today. The locals want to talk to you. They've been on to me. I said you were more or less civilised for a bloke in your game and that you'd come in. I've got one of them on his way now.'

'That wouldn't be Barton of Bellambi, would it?'

'Hardy . . .'

'I'll play. Just give me that much.'

'I remember what a tricky bastard you were, always fucking around to get an edge.'

'You'd do the same in my place.'

'I hope to Christ I'm never there. Okay, this isn't Barton. How long?'

'An hour.'

'Pull your finger out—half an hour.'

He hung up—last-word Aronson.

I found Marisha in her work room fiddling with a tape. I put my arms around her from behind and felt the resistance.

'I have to go,' I said. 'That was the police. Something else I'm working on.'

The stiffness went out of her like wine from a bottle. She somehow managed to twist in my arms, turn and get free of the chair. She leaned into me, her small, firm breasts pressing against my stomach. 'I thought it might be a woman.'

Despite what I'd said earlier, I felt myself responding to the warmth and tautness of her body. 'No,' I said. 'I don't have a woman.'

I got there forty-five minutes later on the dot. The detectives' room at Glebe is upstairs, open plan with a couple of interview rooms off to one side. Nothing fancy. Aronson, in his trademark black leather jacket, was sitting in a corner drinking coffee with a man in a suit. Nice suit, too. He stood as I approached but Aronson didn't.

'Hardy, this is Detective Inspector Ian Farrow up from the 'Gong. Sir, this is Cliff Hardy, licensed private nuisance. I'll leave you to it.'

Farrow and I shook hands and he sat down in the chair Aronson had vacated. I took the other one. Farrow was youngish for his rank with fair hair and a fresh complexion. He looked fit, as if he took exercise and ate the right foods. Social drinker at most. He took out a notebook and looked down at it for a second. When he looked up I was blinking at a stab of pain in the back of my head.

'Something wrong?'

'Took a knock to the head last night. Hurts a bit. What'd you want from me, Inspector?'

'You were in Wollongong yesterday and in the Keira Hotel last night enquiring about Adam Ian MacPherson. You left your card with, ah . . . Margaret Fenton, asking her to give it to him when he came in. She did.'

'That all sounds correct.'

'MacPherson's been murdered.'

I jerked my thumb at Aronson, who was on the phone a few metres away. 'So he told me.'

'You don't seem concerned.'

'I am. I wanted to talk to him, but I never met the man.'

Farrow looked me in the eye and suddenly he didn't seem young and fresh-faced anymore. There were lines of experience around his eyes and mouth and a sceptical frown mark between his eyebrows. 'Didn't you?' he said.

I had to smile. 'Are you new at this?'

'I beg your pardon.'

'The hard stare and the threatening tone. If you really

thought I'd killed him you'd hardly invite me here so politely. And if I had killed him would I be likely to leave him with my card, or be hanging about, having chatted to the barmaid like that?'

'Good point. No, I think we can say we're asking you to help us with our enquiries.'

'That's usually code for being a suspect. You mean in the true sense of the words?'

'Exactly.'

I had no real reason to be concerned. My client wasn't compromised in any way. I gave him a selective version of my investigation for Elizabeth Farmer. Farrow took notes but didn't seem very interested. I couldn't blame him. I didn't mention Matilda's interest in buying the Wombarra block, nor Lucas's hint about why insurance claims are sometimes settled quickly. If there was a connection between MacPherson's death and the Farmer matter, I wanted to see it for myself before I let the police in on it. Unfortunately, Farrow was a good actor and he'd been faking.

'You're full of shit, Hardy. I've spoken to a detective at Bellambi.'

'Barton,' I said.

'Right. He says your client thinks her dad was murdered. You go down and sniff around and the guy who sold the insurance on that particular house gets shot after you shout his name about.'

'Not exactly.'

'I doubt that anything's ever exact with you. You're slippery. But we'll try—what did you want to talk to him about?'

'Look, I was just going by the book. My client hired me to investigate the circumstances of her father's death. The death was by fire. The house was insured. So you talk to the insurers. Routine.'

He consulted his notes. 'You talked to the investigator—Lucas. What did he tell you?'

'Nothing much. He signed off on the claim. Couldn't find anything dodgy. One thing he told me was how to find MacPherson, which was to hang around in that same pub.'

'Sounds to me as if you were just going through the motions.'

There was contempt in every syllable and I struggled to keep my response under control. I studied Farrow closely and decided that he knew he wasn't on firm ground. Out of the corner of my eye I could see Aronson watching us. This wasn't a confrontation I wanted to lose.

'I'm guessing MacPherson was a drunk,' I said as I got to my feet. 'I'm guessing he was sacked by the insurance company and probably had very dirty fingers in lots of pies. You need to find out who killed him. I don't. So unless there's something else, I'm out of here.'

'Intending to go back to Wollongong?'

'Are you offering me a lift?'

'Don't press your luck, Hardy. Obstructing a police investigation is a crime.'

So it is, I thought, but there's nothing to say I had to help it along. I left, nodding to Aronson as I went. I had things of interest to report to Dr Farmer but not all of them reflected well on me—to get both the Bellambi cops, who'd played a part in the fire investigation, and a senior Wollongong policeman offside wasn't good going.

. . .

Glebe doesn't quite have the variety of ethnic food
Newtown boasts, but it's not too bad. After my emotionally
stirring time with Marisha Karatsky and a three-round
no-decision bout with canny Inspector Farrow, I needed
some fuel. I bought a can of Guinness at the bottle shop a
block from the police station and took it into the Italian
joint across the road where I ordered veal parmigiana. It was
the sort of meal I bought to impress women in my brief
student days—with chianti and Peter Stuyvesant, the height
of chic.

By the time I'd finished eating it was after one. I rang
Elizabeth Farmer who told me she could see me between
classes a little after three o'clock. Not enough time to recon-
nect with Marisha. Nothing to do but linger over a couple
of long blacks and think. Trouble was, I was trying to think
of two matters at the same time and as far as I know that
can't be done. So I just drank the coffee.

Dr Farmer had suggested we meet at the coffee shop just
across the Broadway footbridge. Said she needed fresh air at
that time of the day. The air wasn't all that fresh, with the
traffic flowing past twenty metres or so below, but the
breeze was in the right direction at least. I was there first
and saw her walking along beside one of the ivy-covered
walls. In long blue coat, scarf and boots she looked the
part and it occurred to me that Germaine Greer would've
walked along the same road, probably dressed in much the
same way. Forty years ago. This coffee place wouldn't have
existed, nor the footbridge, but not much else had changed.

We went through the she-sits-you-stand routine, and
I asked her what she'd have.

'Long black,' she said. 'I'll be paying, won't I? You being on expenses.'

'I don't always keep the receipts. Might let you off this one.'

The coffee came in plastic cups but tasted okay. She took a drink and leaned back. 'Had to get out of that room. It's a bit claustrophobic.'

'I wouldn't be surprised if there's a touch of asbestos around as well.'

She grinned. 'Thanks. So, Mr Hardy, how do things stand? But first, what happened to your head?'

'What?'

'Your hair's all matted at the back. I notice these things. I look for bald patches, comb-overs . . .'

I shuddered. 'Comb-overs. Yeah, I bumped against a wall. Nothing to do with this.'

'But to do with something. You've got a look in your eye. You're uppish, despite the injury.'

'I thought you were a doctor of philosophy, not—'

'You're right. You're right.' She sipped her coffee. 'Down to tintacks. Shit, what good would tintacks be? Sorry, I'm . . . Never mind, I haven't got long, let's get on with it.'

I filled her in, telling her the things I hadn't told the police. There'd been no need for her to complete the sentence she'd interrupted. Elizabeth was wired, high on something chemical. There was a brightness to her eyes and a sheen to her smooth skin and her hand, as she raised and lowered the coffee cup, wasn't entirely steady. Her body was betraying her. Maybe you needed something chemical to survive in the university scene these days. She unwound the scarf and let it hang down. She'd already undone her coat, and now she sat there in a quite cool

breeze with nothing between it and her except a silk shirt.
But her brain was working and she reacted sharply when
I got to the bit about MacPherson being killed.

'Jesus, is there a connection?'

'Don't know. Possibly not. I'd have to find out more
about him and what happened.'

'How would you do that?'

'I've got ways.'

She accepted that but still shook her head. 'I can't see it.
I can't see some developer killing two people to get hold of
that land. It's all subject to slip, it's honeycombed with mine
workings.'

'So Sue Holland said. There's an entrance on her
property.'

She blinked at the name. 'Mine too. But as well as that,
there's a height limit to any buildings. Where's the profit?'

'Why did Matilda offer to buy it?'

'Just to screw me's my guess. Pick it up cheap. Although
come to think of it, the offer was on the high side. It's a
great spot, as you must've seen.'

I nodded. 'Pretty good. Bit cold under the scarp in
winter I bet.'

'Barbecues, wood fire inside. Lovely.'

'Could the land have any other value?'

She laughed. 'I suppose you could grow a lot of dope
there, but it'd be a bit obvious. The spotter planes go over
all the time and with the yuppies moving in there'd be
dobbers galore. In case you're thinking otherwise, I don't
consider myself a yuppie blow-in. I've been going down
there for more than twenty years.'

'You'll rebuild then?'

'You bet. Something as close to the original as I can.'

She looked at her watch. 'I have to get back. You're not going to stop are you? There *must* be something behind this.'

'Sue Holland said zoning could be changed. It's happened before.'

She shook her head. 'Not down there. No way. Something else.'

'I'll stay with it. I'll run checks on Matilda, find out what I can about MacPherson, see if there's some big money around taking an interest. But . . . no promises.'

'Fair enough.' She stood, formidably tall in her boots, and I immediately thought of Marisha Karatsky, who wouldn't have come up to her shoulder. We shook hands and she wound her scarf back, buttoned her coat. 'And mind your head.'

11

I'd outsmarted myself. The two cases I thought wouldn't amount to much and could be run parallel had turned out to be more involved, both requiring time and attention. And there was the extra factor of the emotional involvement with Marisha. That probably tipped the balance, but I decided that the hunt for Kristina had priority anyway. The question of who wanted the Farmer land, why and what they were prepared to do to get it wasn't going to go away and was unlikely to change shape quickly. Or so I reasoned.

I dug out the material Marisha had provided and looked at the list of Kristina's alleged friends. In my experience, young women with a secret admirer feel the need to confide in someone. I rang Marisha, told her the police business had resolved itself for now, and asked her which of the names she'd given me was most likely to be Kristina's confidante.

'Cliff, it's hard to tell. How would I know?'

'The most mature one. The most . . . experienced, say.'

'I see.' She paused. I could imagine her in her silk smock standing by the phone, her hand up to her tangled hair.

My juices flowed and I realised I wanted to find Kristina, not out of professionalism, but to impress her mother. Not a good reason.

'I think Lucy Kline,' Marisha said. 'I gave you her address. She left school or was expelled, I'm not sure. She has a flat with other young people.'

'I've got it. One more thing. That stuff you were asked to translate by Parnevik. What was it about? Might help me to trace him. I should have asked you before, but we got sidetracked.'

Her throaty laugh was like a caress. 'Skiing. I could follow just enough to know it was about skiing. When am I going to see you, Cliff?'

'Very soon,' I said. 'Probably tonight. I'll try to find Lucy Kline and talk to her and see what comes of that.'

'Good. My daughter is in danger and I have made love to the man who has put her there and the man who is trying to save her. Life is strange, isn't it?'

'It is,' I said.

Lucy Kline's address was in Petersham but I was more interested in Karen Bach. Kristina tucking her name and address away in her hidey-hole had to mean something. Karen Bach's address was in Five Dock, in a street running down to the canal that threads through the area. As I drove I tried to figure out why a place would be called Five Dock when it had no docks at all. I didn't come up with an answer, but with all that's happened to Sydney Harbour since 1788, anything is possible.

The flat was in a nondescript block not far from the canal and the stretch of park running alongside it. Cream

brick, no balconies, aluminium windows, cement paths—
a 1960s suburban dream. Connections of my father, who
were better heeled than him, took this route. They bought
an old house, knocked it down, built the four flats, lived in
one, rented the others. They either died of boredom or got
tired of paying to fix the leaking roofs and dodgy plumbing
and sold out.

There was no security. I went up to the door of flat 2
and rang the bell. The young woman who answered looked
at my licence folder short-sightedly through thick glasses.
She had a paperback book in her hand with a finger
marking her place.

'Really?' she said. 'A private detective?'

'That's right. No gun, no trench coat.'

She giggled. 'Can I help you?'

'Are you Karen Bach?'

'No.'

'Do you know Kristina Karatsky?'

She shook her head.

'Can you tell me where to find Ms Bach? No trouble for
her—a missing person enquiry.'

She pointed towards the canal. 'She's walking her dog.'

'Okay, thanks. What does she look like? What sort
of dog?'

A kind of shadow passed across her face. She was
plain with mousy hair and sallow skin. She was shortish,
neither fat nor thin. She wore a sloppy Joe and baggy
jeans, socks, no shoes. 'Karen's a tall blonde,' she said.
'You'll find her.'

The light was dropping as I walked down to the strip of
green. It made the scene softer, more attractive than it
would look in the clear light of day. There were a few people

around—joggers, dog-walkers, aimless strollers. A tall
blonde woman wearing tight red pants, snowy sneakers and
a faded denim jacket was striding along the path by the
canal with a prancing white poodle on a lead. I like dogs
but I don't like poodles—don't know why.

I trotted across the grass and fell in beside her. 'Ms Bach?'

'Go away,' she said.

'I can't, sorry. I'm a private detective looking for your
friend, Kristina Karatsky. I have to talk to you.'

'She's not my friend. Never was.'

'We still have to talk.' I could handle the pace, but it
was brisk. 'Looks to me like Fifi there needs a rest. I suggest
you slow down.'

That got her attention. 'Her name's Tasha and she could
outrun you any day.'

'No doubt about it, but she must be due to find a tree.
Come to think of it, I am too.'

She laughed and that brought her to a halt. With Tasha
skittering at the end of the plaited lead, she turned and
faced me. She was young, late teens at most, and beautiful,
but there was something older about her. Her big blue eyes
had seen more than they should have.

'Shit,' she said. 'I knew this'd happen one day. An
underage, child molestation, minister of religion thing,
right? That's all I fucking need right now.'

We were standing in the middle of the path with joggers
bearing down on us. I took her arm and steered her towards
a park bench. Tasha tugged at the lead but came along.

'Nothing like that,' I said, lying. 'Nothing to involve
you directly. I just need information about . . . I guess you
know who I mean?'

'Stefan.'

I suppressed a sigh of satisfaction. 'Right. Stefan Parnevik. Do we talk here or back at your flat?'

Inside, the flat was surprisingly well furnished and appointed. It had been thoroughly renovated and re-designed. Tasha had the run of the place so there were dog hairs on the rugs and the sofa and chairs and probably in other places. Karen Bach introduced me to Becky, the flatmate, who promptly disappeared into a bedroom.

'Becky's shy, I'm not. Want a drink, Mr Hardy?'

'Sure.'

'Vodka and tonic okay?'

She'd shed the denim jacket and her figure was on display in a tight fitting top. She sliced a lemon, broke out ice cubes and prepared the drinks like someone who knew what she was doing. She noticed me noticing.

'I did a bar course. Kris did it with me.'

'She's fifteen.'

'So? Here's your drink. Have a seat.'

We sat opposite each other at a low table with a glass top. The drink was excellent. 'What about school?'

'Neither of us was big on school.'

'Her mother—'

She almost snorted and stopped herself because it didn't fit her sophisticated image, an image I was sure she was working at constantly. 'Her mother didn't know shit. Any-way, she's nuts.'

'Why d'you say that?'

She shrugged, reached for a packet of cigarettes on a ledge under the table and lit one. She took a long drag and expelled the smoke theatrically. 'Look, Mr Hardy, I'll come clean with you. I agreed to talk to you because I thought it'd be interesting to meet a private eye. I'm an aspiring actress, presently working as a barmaid, sort of.'

I worked on the drink. A refurbished two or three bedroom flat in Five Dock, however plain the building, wouldn't come cheap these days. Karen Bach, even with a flatmate, wasn't just pulling beers.

She reached to the ledge for an ashtray and butted the two-drag cigarette. 'Topless,' she said. 'Lap dancing.'

'Someone has to do it. Kristina . . . and her mother.'

'Kris talked her way into the course, fake ID and that, but she couldn't get a job. All the makeup and come-on in the world didn't help. Just too fucking young. I did. She freaked. She ripped off my first pay. I told her to fuck off.'

'You said something about her mother.'

'You're working for her, right? Don't. She's a monster.'

'Come on.'

'True. She used Kris to attract blokes. Started when Kris was just a kid. You've seen that place she lives in. How d'you reckon she got that?'

'You tell me.'

She emptied her glass. 'Jesus, I shouldn't be talking about this. I dunno . . . But it's hard stuff to know and hold in.'

I could feel something like a chill starting in my spine and spreading out. 'Tell me.'

'I'll deny I said anything about this if the law gets involved.'

'Right.'

'As I say, she used Kris as bait for blokes to get her jobs and then . . . to blackmail them. She'd be using you the same way, I reckon.'

I sat back and let it hit me hard. Then I thought about it. I was alert, keyed-up. A little alcohol doing no harm to the synapses. 'Her mother steered me to someone named Lucy Kline. Who's she?'

'Fucking hell,' she said. 'A nerd who happened to get caught smoking a joint. Probably her first and last. Kris's mother only ever saw me in school uniform. Kris never let her fucking mother know she knew what was going on. She got all she could out of it herself. She's a better actress than Meryl Streep. Come to think of it, they both are—her and her mother.'

12

As I'd expected, Kristina had talked to Karen Bach about Stefan Parnevik. She hadn't met him but had seen him from a distance.

'Big, fair-haired bloke. Lots older than her, but that never worried Kris.'

'Do you know what he did for a living?'

She thought, or tried to look as though she was thinking. Maybe practising her acting. 'Skiing,' she said. 'Something to do with skiing.'

'No idea where he lived or where his business was?'

She shook her head. 'Sorry. Look, I've got to get to work.'

'Give you a lift?'

'Thanks. No, I've got a car. Hey, that's something. I saw his car. I know cars—silver grey Saab, beautiful.'

I thanked her and got to my feet with my head hurting a little, but whether from the injury or what I'd been told I didn't know. 'Say goodbye to Becky for me.'

'Goodbye from me as well. I don't want to see you again. Hey, you think I'm a dyke?'

I shrugged. 'No opinion.'

'Becky's going to be my manager when I get into movies. She's a fucking genius.'

'Good,' I said. 'We need a few of them the way things are going.'

Karen didn't quite know what to make of that. Tasha was spread out on the imitation leather couch. She lifted her head and watched me all the way to the door.

It was dark by the time I got back to the car. I sat there for a while trying to tell myself that Karen, the wannabe actress, was acting, and that everything she'd told me about Kristina and Marisha was bullshit. Maybe the two young women were still friends, working some kind of rip-off of vulnerable older men. I couldn't convince myself, and when I followed her Honda Civic to a pub in Erskineville that advertised 'topless and titty', I gave the idea away. She wouldn't be working there if she had anything else going.

I drove home in a very confused state. Easy enough to get angry about being taken for a mug if that's what had happened. I tried to keep the anger in check to permit clear thinking. If everything Karen Bach had said was true, then Marisha Karatsky was still playing some sort of game to do with Stefan Parnevik. Had she lost him and wanted him back? Had she suspected already that Kristina was with him and all I had done was confirm it? Was my job just to locate him with evidence of his association with an underage female to allow Marisha to . . . ?

My mood deteriorated as I thought about it. It had been a longish and confusing day, not arduous physically, but taxing just the same. I made myself a meal by defrosting meat I had in the freezer, chopping up some onions and subjecting the mixture to a dose of Clive of India curry powder. I still had a couple of bottles of chardonnay left from my one wine club purchase, since the literature had gone in the bin for its patronising and pretentious tone. I microwaved some pappadums and sat down to it with a big glass of wine and a few more paracetamols. My head was hurting again. I was supposed to see Marisha that evening. How the hell was I going to do that?

Confrontation. Nothing else for it. I finished the meal off with a cup of strong coffee, showered and headed for Dulwich Hill. I wasn't looking forward to the meeting and took the drive slower than I needed to. I buzzed her flat and got no response. Buzzed again, and again. Nothing. I called her number on my mobile and the phone rang and rang. No answering machine. I stood outside the building with frustration and anger mounting inside me.

The parking spaces for the building were unnumbered so I had no way of telling whether she had a car or if it was there or not. I walked along the adjacent street, staring up at the windows. Hers were curtained and dark. I could've hung around, tried to get myself buzzed in by another resident, or maybe slipped in when someone was going in or out. Once in, I could've picked her lock and snooped. Instead, I consigned her and her daughter to hell and drove home. I knocked off the rest of the bottle of white and went to bed.

I don't often dream and when I do I usually forget the content straight off. I remember some though, and the ones I remember have two themes. One is that I'm in danger in a high place. These dreams usually end with me falling or jumping and then I wake up. In others, my father is present. I didn't get on well with him or admire him, and in the dreams he reproaches me the way he did in life. I try to find some common ground with him but it doesn't happen. What Freud or Jung would make of all this I don't know and don't care. So the dream I had where my father criticised me for fucking Marisha Karatsky (though that was a word I never heard him use) didn't surprise me, but it hung disturbingly around through the early part of the morning.

I rang her number several times with no result. Kristina's mobile number had registered on my mobile when she'd rung me after taking the car. I rang it and got the message that the number was no longer in operation. So the Karatskys had quit the stage. I was out a day's pay and a few expenses. No big deal. But being used and deceived, if that's what had happened, rankled. I tried to recapture the quality of the time with Marisha—the sex, the talk, the laughs. It had seemed pretty good, but the more I thought about it, the more it seemed like an act. That intense, that quickly?

I could shrug it off. I'd had worse disappointments and fifteen-year-old Kristina had shown every sign of being able to handle herself in the dodgy world she was in, apparently by choice. I decided to turn my attention to the Farmer matter. That was where the money was, and the questions to be answered, and there was no emotional involvement to muddy the waters.

I got the *Illawarra Mercury* up online. It contained a substantial article on the murder of Adam MacPherson, thirty-three, insurance salesman. The writer's name was

Aaron De Witt and I phoned him at the paper. At a guess, more than fifty per cent of the calls journalists get are from nutters, liars or worse. A good journo can tell pretty quickly whether the caller is worth his or her time. After a few sentences I had De Witt's attention.

'Not much detail on how and where, let alone why,' I said.

'Shotgun up close. What you might call emphatic.'

'Also noisy.'

'Well, up-market townhouse, double glazed, and you know how it is—you hear shots at night, it's probably Bruce or Clint.'

'What about why?'

'We should meet.'

'I'm coming down today. You say where and when.'

'Any preferences?'

'I'd rather not be too close to any police precincts.'

He laughed. He said he was writing a story on the problem with the coast road and would be in the Coalcliff area. We agreed to meet in the Clifton pub at 1 pm, giving me time to pack a few more things than I'd taken the first time and to fit in a quick gym workout. Before I left I rang Marisha's number again with the same result. I had a fleeting, unsettling thought: what if the pair of them were in some kind of danger from Parnevik or someone else? I dismissed it, but it was enough to take the edge off my pleasure at getting out of Sydney.

The Clifton pub sits high above a rocky shore. The coastline is fragile and photographs inside the hotel show that it has changed a lot over the years. The mine that burrowed into the escarpment is now just a coking operation, and the jetty where the coal was loaded was swept away years ago. Most of the houses that once perched on top of the cliff are long gone and the instability problem with the road indicates that changes are still going on. There was a concrete barrier and a boom gate across the road and a high chain link fence with barbed wire further on. With the coast road closed for the couple of kilometres between Clifton and Coalcliff, the locals have to go a long way around to north or south to get to where they used to go directly. The closure had made the Sydney papers and there was a suggestion that house prices in the area could drop as a result. Nobody'd be happy about it.

The weather had taken a turn for the worse and I was wearing jeans, my flannie and a leather jacket and needing every layer. I was early and business wasn't brisk. I studied the photographs of the shoreline and then a set featuring boxers who were from the area or had fought locally in the golden era of Australian boxing—Spargo, Delaney, Patrick and others.

I was nursing a beer on the big back deck that looked straight east to New Zealand when a tall man walked out and ran his eye over the three or four of us rugged outside drinkers. He held a copy of the *Mercury* in one hand and a schooner in the other. I caught his eye and nodded. He must have topped 195 centimetres and a couple of stiff strides brought him to my table.

He stuck out his hand. 'De Witt.'

'Cliff Hardy.' We shook.

'Thing you should know,' he said. 'I'm a recovering alcoholic. This is soda and bitters. I can handle staying here about as long as it'll take you to finish that beer.'

'Okay,' I said. 'You test yourself, right?'

He nodded. 'You've been there?'

An image of Glen Withers, tight as a drum with the effort of not drinking in a drinking environment, came to my mind. 'Friend,' I said.

I proposed that we meet at the Farmer property in Wombarra. It seemed like a good setting for us to exchange information. The way it can in the Illawarra, the weather changed in a few minutes. The sun was shining and the wind had dropped when I reached the gate leading to the Farmer acres. Off with the jacket. De Witt parked his Volvo station wagon carefully by the side of the road but stepped out into thick grass and a soft spot. He was wearing a baggy linen suit over a black poloneck skivvy. Shiny black slip-ons, now rather muddy. He picked his way carefully towards me over the sloppy ground.

'Bit of rain here lately,' I said.

He nodded. 'All we need. A bit more at the right time in the right place and that coast road's history. There's a metre wide crack running for fifty metres on the sea side of the road. Deep, too.'

'Aren't they working on it?'

'Thinking about it.' He cleared his throat, pulled out his cigarettes and lit up. 'But we're not here to talk about the weather or roads, are we?'

'No.'

'Why are we here?'

Insisting it was off the record for now, I elaborated on the little I'd said on the phone, telling him about the Farmer case and how it had led me to MacPherson.

'Or not quite to him,' I said. 'The cops found my card on him and knew I wanted to talk to him.'

'Interesting. Why me?'

'I checked on a few of your stories. Seems to me you've got a pretty good idea of what goes on around here. And reading between the lines in your piece on MacPherson, I reckon you can say a bit more about him than that he was a thirty-three-year-old insurance salesman.'

'You're right there. Now just suppose there's something in all this . . .'

'You've got the inside track.'

'Fair enough.'

We were both leaning on the gate enjoying the pale sunshine. I guessed that De Witt, although his face was lined and grooved, was only in his mid-thirties. But from the tension in his long body and the way he was smoking, he looked likely to die sober in his forties. He gazed out over Elizabeth Farmer's inheritance and shook his head. 'I can't see a development behind it. Your client'll have to get all sorts of permits even to rebuild here.'

'That's what she says, but like I told you, she's had a generous offer from her dad's ex. I thought you might be able to look into whether Matilda Sharpe-Tarleton Farmer has any dodgy connections down here.'

'Speculative investigation?'

'Yeah, like the Watergate burglary.'

He grinned, blew a cloud of smoke and was gripped by a spasm of coughing. I slapped his bony back and when he'd recovered he looked at me with watery eyes. 'I know, I know. And while I do that, what will you be doing?'

'What was MacPherson into—drugs, vice, politics?'

'All of the above.'

'With a few signposts from you, that's where I'll be looking.'

13

De Witt told me that MacPherson was a veteran of the 1991 Gulf War and had been a member of an outlaw bikie gang for a few years after that. Then he'd done a business degree at Wollongong University and had a few jobs in the insurance business before his last position with Illawarra Mutual.

'That job was most likely a cover. MacPherson was almost certainly still involved in drugs. Had too much money for it to be otherwise.'

'You mentioned vice and corruption.'

'No, you did. But they all go together. The pros down here are almost all addicts. So are some of the paedophiles, and some of them're in high places. Put two and two together.'

'All this'd be known to the police?'

'Hard to say. Some of it.'

'I got the impression from Lucas that MacPherson was a bit of a loser, on the skids.'

De Witt shrugged and lit the last cigarette from his packet of plain Camels. He looked anxiously at the soft pack as he crumpled it. 'Probably a pose. They say he could act a lot of parts.'

'You know more about him than you let on in the article. I get the feeling you took an interest before he got killed.'

'Right.'

'So, am I homing in on your story?'

'No, no. I'm glad you're in. Now you can go sniffing around that stuff while I do the safe work.'

As I hoped he could, he filled me in with more information about MacPherson and the underworld of the Illawarra.

'Are you happy to stand back?'

De Witt pressed the butt of his last smoke into the soft ground and turned towards me. His young/old face looked tired. 'Hardy,' he said. 'I'm thirty-six and I feel fifty. I'm off the booze and grass and I have to get off the smokes. I've got a wife and two young kids. I'm looking for a quiet life. Nice editorship here or somewhere else. People who go where you're going down here have a way of turning up very hurt or rather dead.'

De Witt drove off and I climbed the gate. I went past the burnt-out house and further down looking for the track to Sue Holland's land. I'm no country man, but it wasn't hard. Several large stands of lantana had been slashed to open up a path that at one time had been heavily overgrown. Now it was clear enough, showing signs of being walked fairly frequently by someone handy with a machete.

I tramped along, ducking under low branches but in no danger of losing the track, until I emerged at the side of the Holland cottage. I wasn't trying to be quiet and the old dog sussed me out and came towards me with his head up and his tail stiff.

'Fred,' I said. 'Good old Fred. Friend. Friend.'

Fred growled several times and then let out a series of short, sharp barks. Sue Holland came from the back of the house. She looked flustered and upset, maybe angry.

'You again. At least you had the sense not to pat him. He doesn't like people coming from that direction.'

'Sorry,' I said. 'I didn't know that. I didn't mean any disruption. I just—'

'It's all right. I've just had a run-in with some bikie hoons roaring around in one of my paddocks. Arseholes.'

'Bikies, or trail bikes?'

'I know the difference, Mr Hardy.'

'Did they . . . do anything?'

'You mean rape me? I'd like to see them try. I capsicum-sprayed one of them so that he fell off.'

'I didn't hear anything. When was this?'

Her tanned face was pale and perspiration had matted her hair. 'An hour ago. The adrenalin's gone and I'm shaking.'

'Okay. You need to sit down and have a hot drink with plenty of sugar in it.'

'Yuck.'

'Honey then. Something to boost—'

'Mr Hardy, I'm sorry but I think men suck as a species. I'll deal with my body chemistry in my own way. What are you doing here?'

The only way to deal with Sue Holland was to be as direct as she was. 'Who made you the offer for your land?'

'What?'

'You told me Frederick Farmer had had an offer for his

place and so had you. I want to know who made your offer.
If you know who made his, so much the better.'

The dog had taken up a position by her side but he'd
grown tired of the conversation and looked as if he'd like to
head back to his kennel. Sue Holland definitely needed a
rest as well. She put her hand to her forehead and felt the
hair pasted there. 'Jesus,' she said. 'I can't think. Can I get
back to you?'

'Of course. You've got the mobile number. Are you sure
you're going to be all right?'

'I'll be fine. Come on, Fred.' She turned on her heel and
she and the dog went back to the cottage. Birds burst into
song as I moved and I could hear other forms of wildlife
rustling in the scrub. A bit too early for sunbathing snakes,
but I kept an eye out just the same. I followed the gravelled
track back to the road and went up the hill to where the
Falcon was parked. For me, that was enough bushwalking
and country life for one day.

According to De Witt, MacPherson had kept up a kind
of connection with the university, doing odd courses in a
lackadaisical way to give him access to student drug users.
De Witt himself was a part-time tutor in journalism, had
been a recreational pot smoker, and heard grapevine stories
about MacPherson. One of the stories was that, although
MacPherson was married, he had a bikie girlfriend.

'He kept this very dark,' De Witt had said. 'I doubt the
police know about her.'

The woman's name was Wendy Jones and she lived in
Port Kembla.

'When you say bikie . . . ?'

'D'you know the joke Roseanne used to tell when she was a standup?'

I didn't.

De Witt assumed the pose. 'It goes something like this: "Bikers. I hate bikers. They smell, they're dirty, got lice in their hair and beards, they chew tobacco and piss by the side of the road—and that's just the women." Never met her, but from what I hear, that's something like your Wendy. Probably not as grotty.'

De Witt didn't have an address for her but he said there was a dirt track in a waste ground area to the south of Port Kembla where the bikies raced, drank and did the other things bikies do.

'When?'

'Every night, so long as the different gangs aren't actually fire-bombing each other.'

'Hard scene to infiltrate. I've never ridden a motorbike in my life.'

'Oh, plenty of civilians turn up for the product.'

'The cops?'

'Know they're outnumbered and possibly outgunned.'

'Great.'

De Witt had been fairly specific about where the bikie meeting place was located and I wondered whether he might have made the trip there himself in his more toxic days. I drove south keeping an eye on the rear vision mirrors. The last thing I needed was to attract police interest. In fact the more I thought about it, the more sensible it seemed to get a different car. I left the Falcon in a parking station near the central shopping mall in Wollongong, lugged my

bag to a Hertz office and rented a Mitsubishi 4WD station
wagon.

I rang Illawarra Mutual and asked for Carson Lucas, to
be told that he'd gone on leave.

'That's sudden,' I said.

'Is there anyone else who can help you, sir?'

The words, delivered in the meaningless singsong tone
some receptionists use, struck me as funny and I laughed.

'Sir?'

'Nothing. Thank you.'

I waited and it came. 'Have a nice day.'

I sat in the comfortable car with the mobile in my hand
in a strangely thoughtful mood. There was nobody else
who could help me and it seemed somewhat unlikely that
I'd have a nice day. With luck, it wouldn't be too bad.
I checked the *Gregory's* and tried to familiarise myself
with the area south of Wollongong where I'd never been.
The steelworks dominated the map and Lake Illawarra, a
pinpoint on a small-scale map, almost filled a page of
the directory. The NRMA accommodation guide, another
essential accessory, showed that the area wasn't well off
for motels, but one at Warrawong seemed like the closest
to where I was headed, had the necessary facilities, and
wouldn't make Dr Farmer have to apply for promotion.

I drove to the motel, checked in, bought a hamburger
nearby and ate it with a can of beer from the mini-bar. Two
cans of beer. Then I poured boiling water on two of
the Nescafé coffee sachets, producing a strong cup. I drank
two cups while I scribbled notes on my day's work, connected up names and places and snippets of information
with arrows and dotted lines and peppered the whole
diagram with question marks. I have a collection of these

diagrams going back many years and I don't know what good they do, if any. But I still make them.

Port Kembla and parts south aren't well lit at night and I frequently had to consult the directory by torchlight to make sure I was keeping in the right direction. It took a while with quite a few false turns and dead ends, but eventually I located the bikies' sacred site—a large area that looked like a dried-up lake bed or perhaps a filled-in quarry. I got there more by tracking sight and sound than anything else. The area was a couple of hectares all told and a figure eight dirt track had been graded into existence and confirmed over time by thousands of spinning, skidding wheels. The track was lit by the headlights of twenty or more 4WDs parked at intervals. Riding around that surface in company with others, taking the scarcely banked bends at speed and coming in and out of shadows seemed to me like a good way to break something, from an ankle to a neck.

When I arrived a dozen bikes were in action. They were roaring, and there were at least fifty more lined up ready to roar. There was more leather and denim and greasy hair than at the Altamont Speedway in 1969, and a good scattering of what De Witt called civilians as well. Some long hairs, some baldies, some boozers, some pot heads. I was in my jeans and flannie and, having a heavy beard, I had a strong stubble sprouting. I also had a plastic-looped six pack. I got out of the car and began to wander around, swigging from a can and trying not to stumble over the discarded cans and bottles or slip on the oil slicks. There was no security that I could see. Again, De Witt seemed to have got it right. This was a no-go zone for the forces of law and order and respectability.

Within half an hour I was approached four times: twice by buyers and twice by sellers. I fended them off until I decided my presence would look suspicious. The fifth approach was from a man in leather pants, high-laced hiking boots and an Afghan jacket that looked to date back to the time when people wore Afghan jackets.

'Lookin' for something, dude?' he said in an accent that might've been American. I had to lean down closer to hear him over the revving of the bikes.

'Could be.' I detached a can from the loop and handed it to him.

'Thanks. Pills, pot or pussy?'

I laughed and he took me by the arm and led me to a shadowy spot behind an ancient Land Cruiser whose head-lights were dimming.

'What the fuck're you doing here?' he hissed.

'What?'

'You're a cop. It sticks out like dog's balls.'

'Don't know what you're on about.'

'You're in the way. Sorry, but I've gotta do this.'

He raised his can as if to drink from it and that's the last movement I registered. What followed was a blur and a bump and the loud, flickering, petrol-smelling scene slipped away from me as I went down a long slope into a quiet, dark place.

14

When I came around I was sitting in the passenger seat of a Land Cruiser, seatbelt on, depleted six pack at my feet. As far as I could tell, nothing was broken and nothing hurt more than usual. The man in the Afghan jacket was sitting next to me, smoking. The smoke made me cough.

'How d'you feel?' The doubtful American accent was gone.

'Shithouse, at being taken down so easily.'

'You were off guard, Mr Hardy, and I've had the training. Sorry I took you for a cop, but you had the look. Too much of the look.'

'So why . . . ?'

'Try to work it out.'

I looked him over and thought about it. Almost too good to be true, the way he looked, and the ease with which he'd handled me suggested intensive training.

'Undercover?'

He shrugged. 'You said it, not me.'

My wallet was sitting on the dashboard in front of me, lying open. I'd left it under the seat of the Mitsubishi. This guy knew his business. When I was sure I could move, I looked out to right and left and then straight ahead. Blackness all around. I took the wallet, closed it and stuffed it in the pocket of my shirt.

'Okay, you know who I am and I suppose I know what you're doing, or what you suggest you're doing. Undercover, sure. Easy to say. Trouble is, you've probably got no way of proving it.'

'I could've turned you over to the bikies. They don't make much distinction between private detectives and cops.'

Probably true. I leaned down and pulled a can from the loop. My finger was clumsy in the ring pull but I managed. The beer was still cold so not too much time had elapsed. Good detecting. Could've looked at my watch. The period of unconsciousness had scrambled me a little. I drank some more beer and he took a long drag on his cigarette.

'So where do we go from here?' I said.

'Your car's parked behind us. You piss off back to wherever you came from.'

'Maybe we could help each other.'

'I put in a call on you, mate. You tend to help yourself first and foremost.'

I drank some more beer to get rid of the metallic taste of the first swigs. The taste persisted. It felt as if I could taste my teeth although there's no metal in them these days. Ceramic. 'Private enterprise,' I said. 'Want a beer?'

He crushed out his smoke in the ashtray and accepted a can. His age was hard to guess under the stubble and with the hair. His fingernails were black-rimmed and he smelled of tobacco, marijuana and motor oil. He looked the real thing, semi-feral, but there was an edginess about him, an alertness under the grunge.

'I'm investigating a suspicious death down here and there's been a murder since. I—'

He made an impatient gesture after cracking the can. 'I know what you're doing. I told you I put in a call.'

'To Barton in Bellambi or Farrow in Wollongong?'

He took a long drink and grinned. The beer, just having it in his hand, was relaxing him and I realised how tightly wound he'd been. Still was. 'You're not popular with either of 'em.'

'Being popular's not my go. I think there's something big going on down here. Maybe it's in the planning stage, but there's some money on offer and I think Adam MacPherson's murder's got something to do with it. You must know he was dealing . . . supplying might be a better word. Supply suggests a source.'

'They say you're a talker, but I haven't heard anything yet.'

He'd downed most of the can and slid a little lower in the seat. Earlier, he'd been darting looks out into the night. Fewer of them now.

'Yes you have,' I said. 'You're major crimes or drug squad. Maybe both. Probably with some Internal Affairs briefing as well. You know manufacture and distribution are being . . . facilitated down here.' I pointed a finger out into the darkness, although whether in the right direction or not I had no idea. 'That was a no-go zone within ten miles of the Wollongong CBD. Come on.'

'Miles,' he said.

'Call me old fashioned.'

He swilled the can and lifted it to his ear to judge the amount left. A cautious drinker, or possibly an under-cover technique. 'Okay, say you have some idea of what might be going on. How can you help?'

I shook my head. 'How you can you help *me*?'

'Jesus, Hardy. Ten more minutes back there in that fuckin' flannie with the swinging dick six pack and the ex-army strut and you'd have been bent over a Honda being asked questions with a bike chain.'

I had to laugh—partly acknowledgment of a truth, partly embarrassment. 'I think if I can talk to a certain person I can get a bit further inside what might be going on. If you're the shit-hot undercover guy you come across as, you just might know her.'

'Try me.'

'Wendy Jones.'

He emptied his can and crushed it, probably an obligatory gesture in the circles he'd been moving in. 'I know her,' he said. 'I think we'd better have a proper talk. Where're you staying?'

I told him and he said he'd get me back on a road I'd recognise and then follow me to the motel. Handed me my keys. I asked him how he managed to get my car to where it was without anyone asking questions.

'Most of 'em are either too pissed to notice or too busy watching their bikes or their backs. You wouldn't believe the fights that go on. Anyone noticing would most likely think I was stealing it. Give me a cheer. You all right to drive?'

I drove super-cautiously. I had a certain amount of alcohol inside me, a recent head wound, and having the blood supply to your brain cut off by a commando hold can do things to your vision and perception. But there was very little traffic and his dim headlights behind me were oddly comforting. I pulled into the parking bay at the motel and watched him drive on without hesitation. Just what I'd have done in his place. I went in and filled the jug, put instant coffee in two cups and set out the bottle of brandy I'd nicked from Jason Garvan in Paddington.

A soft knock came on the door. He must've circled the block a couple of times. I opened up and he came in with a lit cigarette in his hand.

'You mind?' he said.

I recognised it for what it was—a pre-emptive strike. 'No,' I said. 'You stay in character.'

'Hey, I smoked before I went undercover.'

I put a saucer on the table as an ashtray. 'Aren't you going to look around for bugs?'

'Let's stop pissing around.' He noticed the cups and the bottle as he ashed his cigarette. 'That looks like a good idea.'

I poured boiling water over the instant, filling the cups to two-thirds. I spiked mine and pushed the bottle towards him as I sat down. He topped his cup up and took a seat, butted the cigarette.

'Wendy Jones,' I said.

He took a strong pull on the spiked coffee and sighed. 'That's good. That grog costs a mint. How come you've got it to splash about?'

'It's a long story, and let's stop pissing around. Wendy Jones?'

'Yeah, I was probably going to wave you goodbye until you came up with Wendy. I've had an interest in her for a while and it seems she's just become even more interesting recently. So, you tell me why you know about her and I'll think about telling you what I know.'

'Hard bargain.'

He shrugged. 'Good liquor, this, but it won't change anything.'

I drank some more coffee and did some thinking. What I had to say was pretty thin and might not extract anything from him. I felt I had to shore up my position a bit before spilling my guts. 'Look, I've been running into actors and poseurs and people who aren't what they seem since I got into this thing. You're in the mix with that phoney Yank accent. I'm still not sure you're what you say you are and I don't even have a name to call you by. I'm considering telling you to drink your coffee and fuck off.'

He grinned, drained his cup and poured himself a slug of the brandy. 'And then what? Go back there again to look for Wendy?'

'Maybe. Better disguised, eh? Get myself an Afghan jacket and dirty fingernails. Smell of dope.'

'You wouldn't find her.'

'So you say.'

He moved quickly and flexibly, proving he was younger than he looked. He unlaced his right boot and slid his hand down inside a sock that gave off a smell of sweat and decay. He pulled out a card, looked at it for a long minute with an expression I couldn't interpret. Reluctance? Doubt? Then he showed it to me—a police warrant card—with just a touch of pride coming into that worn, strain-racked face.

'Detective Constable Thomas Purcell,' he said. 'I can't remember the last fuckin' time I said that out loud.'

I peered at the card. I'd seen too many of them not to know that it was genuine. 'Okay, Tom,' I said. 'you're on your way to being an unsung hero of the war against drugs if you stay alive. Great, until they change the laws, which they'll have to do sooner or later.'

He slumped in his chair and put his foot back in his boot but didn't lace it up. 'The word is our Wendy's come in to some serious money.'

15

Purcell said he knew about the connection between Wendy Jones and the late Adam MacPherson but his information was that they'd split up very recently. He was interested to hear that her name had come up in my investigation of the death of Frederick Farmer.

'I don't suppose you'll tell me who told you Wendy and MacPherson were on together.'

'No. Not somebody connected to the sticky side.'

'So it's your call. Your infallible judgement.'

'That's right, but I'm not too happy about it. The guy who processed the insurance claim, the one I spoke to, has suddenly gone on leave. The guy he put me on to and I didn't speak to is dead. I'm not too keen on mentioning names.'

'You don't trust me?'

I looked at him, sitting in his grotty clothes with his unlaced boot, drinking brandy from a cup in a cheap motel. The look on his face told me he was seeing much the same picture. We both laughed.

'Wendy's in Sydney,' he said. 'I'm told she's staying at the Novotel—Darling Harbour.'

'She must've cleaned up her act. I'm told she was the original bikie moll.'

'Yeah, she is that, but you can cover tatts and she'd scrub up pretty well if she wanted to.'

'She ride her Harley?'

He shook his head and lifted his cup in an ironic salute. 'BMW, bought today. I've been wondering about it, but these people can get very flush, very quickly. Of course, Wendy knows people. Probably got it cheap.'

'But I've given you something to think about?'

He nodded. 'Just what I needed.'

We kicked it around for a while longer over a little more of Jason's brandy. After he left I reflected that Purcell was the first cop I could recall who didn't tell me to keep my nose out of things. All he said was to be careful. But he was a different kind of cop.

If there's anything lonelier than a cheap motel room in the suburbs at dead of night I don't know of it. Maybe a solitary confinement cell at the Bay in the old days, but I hadn't had the pleasure. I was a bit high on the brandy with nothing much in my stomach to process it, and from feeling that the contact with Purcell had been useful, but coming down fast. There was a chance I could learn something, directly or indirectly, from Wendy Jones to throw some light on Frederick Farmer's death. Dr Elizabeth struck me as a stayer and she might want me to pursue the matter as far as I could. That is, into the sort of danger Farrow and Purcell had hinted at. Okay with me, in fact very okay. I'd long ago come to agree with Cyn and others after her that I could cope better with the dangerous than with the mundane. Dullness, boredom, alcohol would kill me quicker than bashings or bullets.

But, lying half drunk on a lumpy bed in a crummy motel under a low watt light, it was thoughts of Marisha Karatsky that were bringing me down.

In the morning, just before checkout time, I phoned De Witt at the *Mercury*. 'You survived it,' he said.

'No worries. Any luck on Matilda?'

'Not really, but there's one funny thing. I ran the name past a couple of people here and the social page woman said it rang a bell. She's checking some of her back stories and columns.'

'That is a bit strange. My understanding was that she never came near the Wombarra place. I'm surprised to learn she was ever down here at all.'

'Well, let's see if there's anything to it. How did you get on with the bikies?'

I was concerned to protect all my sources of information, and it was getting tangled. Hard to remember who I'd told what. I said I had some leads to follow but nothing solid yet. He caught the hesitation and evasion.

'We had a deal, remember? I hope you're not backing out.'

'The deal stands. You know one of the differences between your game and mine?'

'Tell me.'

'I've learned to have patience, lots of patience.'

I checked out, returned the Mitsubishi and carried my bag back to the parking station. I was accumulating a decent set of receipts for Dr Farmer. The morning was bright with a mild wind promising a spell of decent weather. I decided to get a small workout by climbing the four flights of stairs to my level rather than taking the lift. I remembered Bob Hawke saying he hated jogging and got exercise by walking briskly and swinging his heavy brief-case. Seemed to work for him.

The level was for overnight and longer parking and there was a scattering of cars. My plan was to get onto the highway as quickly as possible to minimise the chance of Barton's boys checking me for bald tyres or defective wipers, both always a possibility. I unlocked the passenger door and slung the bag inside. I reached across to lift the button on the driver's door and felt cold metal press hard behind my ear.

'Don't turn around, Hardy. Just take a deep breath.'

Despite myself, I did what the voice said.

'That's right. Now, feel this.'

The metal moved against my skin—sharp, round, wide.

'Shottie?' I said.

'Right. Double sawn-off. You're going to drive and I'm going to sit behind you with this somewhere around the base of your neck. Maybe not quite touching. Understand?'

'Yeah.'

'Okay. Driver's side keeping your eyes down, reach over and open the back door. Don't look around. Get in, start the car and head for the exit—slowly.'

'Do I put my seatbelt on?'

The shotgun dug savagely into my neck. 'What you do is drive and keep your fuckin' mouth shut.'

I did what the voice said. The Falcon, after sitting cold for nearly twenty-four hours, was reluctant to start.

'Am I allowed to give it some choke?'

He was behind me now with the back door closed. I couldn't feel the gun, but that didn't do anything to reduce the sweat running down my face and breaking out in other places.

'Just get it started or everything stops for you right here.'

The engine coughed, caught, and I nursed it to a healthy purr. 'I'll have to get out to pay.'

'It's been taken care of,' he said. 'Drive!'

I snuck a quick look in the rear vision mirror and saw nothing—taped over. He knew his stuff. I drove down the ramps and the boom gate lifted and we were out on the road.

'Straight ahead and don't do any smart thinking. You're dead in a second and I'm out and off and anyone in my way is collateral damage.'

I drove, obeying his directional instructions. What he said was probably true about being able to get clear and, in any case, it wouldn't matter to me if he did or not. We were heading for the rough land surrounding the sewerage works. From my earlier reading of the map I recalled that it ran partly alongside the golf course. Sewerage plants are pretty much automated with not many workers around, and, unless it was a competition day, not too many golfers would be out. This guy would've checked on that. A shot-gun had seen Adam MacPherson off, and here was one just centimetres from my spinal cord. The sweat was running off me now. The seatbelt hung loose over my shoulder—I wasn't that dumb.

Traffic thinned down to nothing. His sharply barked directions were taking us along empty roads with cyclone fences and bits of industrial plant with no one about. It was the worst of places and the best of places. I made the decision: I swung the wheel and hit the kerb. The bump pulled the shotgun barrel away from my head giving me the time I needed. I hit the brake and threw myself against my bag and the passenger door. What the guy behind didn't know was that the passenger door catch was buggered and would open at a touch. I went through the door with the bag ahead of me, clutching it to break my fall. It partly worked, but I hit hard and felt the wind go out of me as the car careened ahead, out of control.

I rolled and sucked in air. I unzipped the bag and groped for the .38 Smith & Wesson I'd brought along with other accessories. I found it with sweaty fingers and struggled to get my bearings. The Falcon had stalled with its nose buried deep in a stand of lantana. It was fifty metres away. The back door opened and he stepped out, clutching his chest. No seatbelt in the back—a nasty thump. He was a blur at that distance with the sweat running into my eyes. Big. Dark. Beard? Denim? He still had the sawn-off and he pointed it in my direction. Took a few steps.

I fired a shot over his head and he stopped. I moved closer, two hands on the revolver and slightly crouched. At forty metres, a pistol is problematic unless in the hands of an expert, but a sawn-off shotgun is as useless as a tooth-pick. He didn't panic. He fired both barrels in my direction and the shot threw up dirt not too far in front of me. He scrambled under some bushes bordering a creek and moved quickly away. I went after him with the gun in my hand, but I was winded and hurting and he had the greater incentive. I stopped and watched him wade across the shallow creek that ran through the golf course. He climbed out, muddy, before smoothly jogging down the ideal running surface of the closely cut fairway.

16

I limped back to the car with the adrenalin starting to recede, thinking that this had been a very close call. If I hadn't had the gun in the bag, if I hadn't had the bag on the front seat, if the passenger door catch hadn't been dodgy . . . The car was undamaged, maybe a few more scratches on the hood where it had run into the lantana. I started the engine, reversed and drove back to the bag. I collected the stuff that had spilled, shoved it inside and headed off. A .38 doesn't make a very loud report but a shotgun does and I didn't want to be hanging around if anyone came to investigate.

I made some turns and was on a street leading away from the water and the golf course before I realised that I was driving with no rear vision. I stopped and stripped the tape from the mirror. The street was quiet and I sat for a while letting its peaceful ordinariness soothe me. The brandy bottle had rolled clear of the bag. A few swigs left. I soothed myself some more. My heart rate slowed to near normal and I began to take notice of details. My flannel shirt was dirty and ripped at the shoulder where I'd hit the ground. Another item of expense for Dr Farmer. Also one

.38 round . . . I realised that I wasn't thinking straight and felt a sudden surge of panic. What if the guy who'd jumped me had backup? Ridiculous. I closed my eyes and counted to ten.

It's one thing to be threatened, attacked, whatever, because you have something someone else wants or know something someone doesn't want you to know. When you believe you don't have or know anything dangerous it makes it harder to know what steps to take. But when you're being paid, there's really only one option—backing out completely (tempting after the shotgun episode), isn't on. Only thing is to go all out to get the dangerous item of knowledge and use it any way you can. My interest in the connection, whatever it was, between Frederick Farmer's death, the insurance on his land and elements in the Wollongong underworld was at the heart of the matter. And my only way forward was to take a close look at Wendy Jones.

I was back at Waterfall when my mobile rang. Law abiding citizen, and not sure how far Barton of Bellambi's writ ran, I pulled over to take the call. Reception was good; Purcell, the undercover cop I'd given my mobile number to, came in loud and clear.

'Where are you, Hardy?'

'On my way back to Sydney, a bit battered and bruised.'

'How's that?'

I told him what had happened and he whistled, an unpleasant noise over the phone. 'You see him?'

'Not up close. Bikie, possibly. What's this call about?'

'Thought you might appreciate a bit more on Wendy.'

'All you've got. Thanks.'

He read off the registration number of her red BMW. I scrabbled in the glove box detritus for a ballpoint and wrote it down. 'Okay. Got it.'

'She's gone up to gamble. That's her thing whenever she gets her hands on any money. Look for her at the casino.'

I groaned. 'Not at Randwick?'

'Wendy's a night owl.'

'Ah, it'd help to know what she looks like.'

'I've got a picture somewhere. You'll know her. I'll scan it in. Give me your email address.'

I gave it to him and could hear the clatter of computer keys—your modern undercover guy. 'Any idea where the money came from?'

'What's a Beemer cost these days, even second hand? Twenty grand? More? I wouldn't know. And a splurge in Sydney? Another ten? It's a big score from somewhere but I haven't a clue. Gotta go. Good luck, Hardy.'

I drove on with plenty to think about and an aching body in need of some TLC. Nothing in sight. My phone rang again. This time it was Dr Farmer asking me to call on her at her place in Newtown. Why not? It was on my way and I could show her my ragged shirt as evidence that I'd been out and about on her behalf.

Her house was about half the size of the one Matilda Sharpe-Tarleton lived and worked in, but that didn't make it small. Those single-storey, narrow-fronted terraces can open up to something spectacular inside and hers did. She met me at the door. She wore a tracksuit and had recently showered so that her hair was still spiky and wet. She looked healthy but troubled. A set of golf clubs rested against the wall halfway down the passage.

'I played this morning in the comp,' she said as we moved down towards a big, skylighted area where a lot of money had been spent.

Golf courses weren't my favourite places at the best of times and particularly not today, but I made a polite response. She had coffee percolating. She poured two mugs full and we sat down under the skylight. The back of the house was all timber and glass and her tiny bricked courtyard was a riot of plants. Wide pine steps ran up to a mezzanine where I'd bet there was a queen-size bed.

I took a swig of coffee. 'Great house.'

'We like it. Mr Hardy, I was all set to go off to work when Sue Holland called in here.'

'Is that unusual?'

'Very, and thank Christ Tania wasn't here. You probably gathered that Sue and I had a thing going some time ago. Well, I met Tania and it went wrong and Sue's been angry and sad and all that. Difficult at times.'

I nodded and worked on the excellent coffee.

'At first I thought she was going to go over it all again. How she'd loved me and I'd betrayed her and all that. But she didn't. She was sort of apologetic. She's accepted an offer on her property at Wombarra.'

That got my attention. 'I got the impression she loved the place, couldn't live without it.'

She stared out at her sunlit greenery and I had the feeling she was reliving old memories, some good, some bad. She gulped down coffee and got the focus back. 'I'd have said the same. She didn't tell me the figure but she said it was just too much to refuse. She can relocate in the area with money to spare.'

'Did she say who the offer was from?'

'Some solicitor or other. I don't think she mentioned a name. I don't think Matilda could be behind it. I doubt she'd have the sort of money Sue was talking about or would want to spend it that way.'

'Does it set you thinking?'

'You mean would I sell for enough money? No, not if it's got anything to do with killing my dad.'

'It could have. It sort of ties in with—'

She cut me off. 'There's more. She asked me to tell you that she's been working on that impression she had of the person hanging around Dad's place. You remember?'

'Sure.'

'She says she now thinks it was a woman. A sort of bulked-up woman. She stressed that this wasn't some dyke fantasy. You asked her about a vehicle, she says.'

'Right.'

Elizabeth Farmer pushed her damp hair back from her striking face. 'I don't know where all this clarity of recall's come from, maybe from suddenly becoming rich, but she says she heard a motorbike start up after she'd seen this . . . person. You don't look surprised, Mr Hardy.'

I finished my coffee and fingered the rents in my dirty shirt. 'I've been dealing with bikies down there for the last twenty-four hours, thirty-six, maybe. One friendly, most not. I'm not surprised.'

'You got hurt again? I don't—'

'It's all right. My pride mostly. There's something very strange going on in the Illawarra, Dr Farmer, and you've put me right in the middle of it.'

'I'm sorry.'

'No, that's not right. Don't say that. You still want to find out why your father died?'

'I do.'

'So do I, and I've got an ally or two.'

We sat quietly for a few minutes in those up-market surroundings. My thoughts drifted to Marisha Karatsky and the only moments of comfort I'd had since this whole thing started.

She broke in. 'I can tell you something—if Sue Holland says she heard a motorcycle engine you can believe it. She was a motorbike dyke in her day.'

'I believe it,' I said. 'Tell me, what does Tania do?'

'She's an accountant. Why?'

'I need someone to go to the casino with me. An accountant sounds right.'

I explained about Wendy Jones and the possibility of finding out, through her, what might be going on down south.

She made a face. 'Why can't I go?'

The last time I'd taken a client into what might be called an operational situation, the client had been shot and later abducted. I could hardly tell Dr Farmer that, so I fell back on not involving a client at the sharp end as a professional principle. I asked her if Tania would be willing.

'She'd love it. She complains about the dullness of her job.'

'She knows about all this?'

'Of course. We're married.'

It was said as a challenge but I didn't respond. I knew that same sex weddings were going on all the time and that they probably had the same ups and downs as the other kind and de facto set-ups. Downs and yet more downs in my own case.

'Ask her as soon as she comes in. Tonight would be best.'

'It won't be dangerous?'

'No.'

'She'll do it, I know she will. But just supposing she won't, what would you do?'

I shrugged. 'Hire a professional. That'd cost you more money.'

'So you . . . haven't got anyone . . . ?'

'No.'

'Why's that?'

After the events of the morning I wasn't inclined to go down this road. 'It doesn't happen,' I said. 'And when it does, it doesn't last.'

'That's bleak.'

I shrugged again and got to my feet. 'I'll wait for your call. If it's a go, Tania should wear something smart and you should give her some gambling money.'

She smiled as she moved to escort me out. 'I sometimes wish I'd studied psychology instead of linguistics. This is all very interesting.'

Interesting, I thought. Sure, with a couple of people dead and the welts from the prod of a double barrel sawn-off shotgun smarting on my neck. I kept moving and didn't say anything.

'Do you wish you'd done something different, Cliff? Another profession?'

I didn't even have to think. 'Yes and no,' I said.

17

My reasoning was this: the casino had good people and any security man worth his salt would take a close look at someone like me. They might even have me on file, with a photo or video or both, after some of the matters I'd dealt with over the years. If I turned up with a female partner the temperature would drop and she might even be useful in getting me close to Wendy Jones.

As I headed for home, I tried to remember what Tania looked like from the glimpse I'd caught on the street. That's if it *was* Tania, and Elizabeth Farmer wasn't sharing herself about. Blonde, I thought, suede coat. An accountant might be a good companion to go gambling with, but what would you talk to her about? The only accountant I knew was my own and our contact mostly consisted of him telling me what to do and how slack I was about keeping documents.

There was the usual build-up of mail after an absence, mostly inconsequential, and a stack of phone messages, mostly ignorable. The house felt plain and dowdy after the opulence of my client's place but that's probably how I like it. Unlike several women I've known, my habit is to unpack completely on getting home. Dirty clothes in the wash, other stuff back where it belongs. My ex-wife Cyn was capable of stepping over her unpacked bag for weeks, taking what she needed out of it piece by piece.

I showered, applied some antiseptic cream to my scraped shoulder, put on a tracksuit and sneakers and went for a walk. The apartment development at the end of Glebe Point Road was just about ready for the well-heeled owners to move in on their water views. I turned off and did a long circuit through Jubilee Park, over the bridge and back up around Harold Park. The pub has gone and I wondered how much longer the pacing could continue. It seemed like time was passing it by. Up the Wigram Road hill and back home. A couple of kilometres and forty-five minutes of time out. I didn't think about Frederick Farmer or Adam MacPherson or Wendy Jones or Marisha Karatsky.

There was a message with an attachment on the computer from Purcell. The message asked me to scrub the whole lot once I'd looked at it. The attachment was a photograph of Wendy Jones in the company of a gang of bikies. She was in the middle, astride her bike, and looked completely at home. At a guess she was in her mid to late twenties. Her face was arresting—high cheekbones, bony nose, thin lips. The quality wasn't good enough for me to tell the colour of her eyes below heavy, dark brows. Her hair was mid-blonde, drawn back in a bikie ponytail. Slap on the makeup, change the colour and arrangement of her hair, put her in a dress and she could be transformed. But I wouldn't have any trouble recognising her—the photo was sharp enough with the light coming in from the right direction to show that she had a winking jewel implanted in both of her front teeth. I could hear Purcell laughing.

Dr Farmer called to confirm that Tania was a starter. At 10 pm, in my only dark suit with a collar and tie and well-shined shoes, I parked outside the bijou terrace in Newtown. Dr Farmer ushered me in and introduced me to Tania Vronsky. She was the woman I'd seen in King Street— medium height, short blonde hair, an athletic body. She wore a black silk dress with a cream jacket, medium heels.

We shook hands. I said, 'Ms Vronsky' and she said, 'Mr Hardy.'

Elizabeth Farmer snorted. 'It's going to look bloody funny the two of you walking around calling each other Ms and Mr. His name's Cliff.'

'Hello, Cliff. Thanks for the invitation.'

'A pleasure, Tania.'

'Let's have a drink,' Elizabeth Farmer, who'd obviously already had a few, said. 'Put you both in the mood.'

She had a bottle of champagne open and the glasses ready. She poured, a little unsteadily. 'Good luck,' she said as she handed the drinks around. 'Tell me all about it after, darling.'

In the car, I said, 'She's not too happy about this, is she? D'you want to back out?'

'Shit, no. I love her dearly, but sometimes she's too clingy. This is a godsend. I need some space. Just a bit. For now.'

I started the car. She leaned back and sighed. I drove in silence for a while, threading through the traffic towards Broadway.

'D'you think you could stop so I can get cigarettes, Cliff? It's another no-no at home, but it'd be in character in a casino, right?'

The casino was part of a complex on Darling Harbour. I'd been to a Van Morrison concert in the entertainment centre nearby and I'd eaten in one of the associated restaurants, but I'd never been inside the real money-spinner, the casino. I'd been in others though, and knew what to expect— over-the-top bad taste décor and an arrangement of lights and mirrors that made you think you'd entered another universe. I wasn't wrong: the entrance had lights in the floor and spouting water up glassy walls. Inside the look was something between a tropical island and an Arabian tent— glass, steel and plastic thrown together with a few million watts. Pink dominated, followed by yellow and pale blue.

'Jesus,' Tania said as she took it in. 'Whose idea was this?'

'Probably a committee and based on a study of the sort of thing that most numbs the mind.'

She shot me a look. 'Liz said you weren't dumb.'

'Thanks.'

'Sorry, that sounded patronising. I just . . .'

'You just expect someone in my trade to be thick, physically good, but thick.'

'I said I was sorry.'

'It's okay. What we do is, we get some chips and have a bit of a play. Then I drift around and take a look at this and that.'

'Is your plan really that vague?'

'No, I've got a miniature camera and I'm going to take pictures of who she's with—if she shows. Have to be careful. It's not something the management'd like. D'you know how to play blackjack?'

'I've seen the Bond movies. How does a girl get a drink?'

Strange to say, we really got into it. We placed our drink orders with the circulating waiters and lined up at the blackjack tables and roulette wheels over the next hour and a half. I won and she lost, then she won and I lost. Way it goes. Tania struck up a conversation with another woman and they went off to play the pokies. I drew the line at that. I did it a bit in the old days when you could kid yourself pulling the lever took skill, but the button pressing doesn't do anything for me.

As I moved around, I registered the security guys trying not to be registrable in their smart suits and short haircuts. One or two of them looked me over closely, but I kept checking back with Tania and they evidently decided I was harmless. I helped the impression along by acting as though the drink was getting to me whereas in fact I was going very slowly on spritzers. The crowd built up steadily so that by midnight the noise and the smoke and the joy and despair were at a high level, and that's when Wendy Jones made her entrance.

No other word for it. She sailed in with a big, dinner suited guy on either side. She'd got the hair tamed and turned to platinum. Her red dress was short and tight and low-cut and the white silk jacket wasn't designed to conceal anything. Light bounced off the jewels in her teeth when she smiled and she smiled a lot. They ordered drinks, loaded up with chips, and headed for a blackjack table. Palming the camera and mostly hidden by one of the Parthenon-type pillars, I got off a few shots of the threesome.

I kept behind them after that and hung around on the fringes of a group that formed around a roulette wheel Wendy had evidently decided to make her own. She installed herself with one of her retainers sitting beside her while the other stood at her back. She had a full glass of champagne and a packet of cigarettes and a lighter to hand. Her piles of chips wouldn't have disgraced Kerry Packer. She started to play and people started to watch and follow her because she was betting and winning big. The game is essentially boring, only the money makes it interesting, and the more money, the more interesting it gets.

I began to wonder why Wendy hadn't opted for the high roller rooms where the sort of cash she was laying out now was more acceptable. Then it became clear. From what I'd been told, the gambling in those rooms is cold and clinical, almost mathematical. No audience, no perform-ance, no drama. That wasn't Wendy's style. She played to the crowd, smiling broadly with her glinting teeth when she won and ordering more bubbly, and groaning and seeking sympathy when she lost. It was a good show and the casino wouldn't object as long as she didn't raise the stakes too high, because the people playing off her were mostly losing.

With her chips piled high, a fresh cigarette alight and a full glass to hand, the time came for her to make an important bet. There was a lull, almost as if the whirring pokies had fallen silent for a second, the muzak had died and the glasses had stopped clinking. The guy standing

behind Wendy spoke loudly, as though the background
noise was still high.

'Lay it on, Wendy!'

The croupier called for bets, Wendy slid her chips forward, the wheel spun, the noise mounted again, but I was
frozen back in that momentary lull. The voice I'd heard
was the one that had come from behind me that morning,
accompanying the bite of the sawn-off shotgun behind
my ear.

18

I located Tania at one of the banks of poker machines. She was smoking, playing her machine but also deep in conversation with the woman I'd seen her with earlier. I eased between them.

''lo, Cliff. How's it going?' Her smile was wide, her voice was loud, she was on the way to being drunk.

'Tania, you've been terrific but you're going to have to make your own way home.'

'You're dumping me. You get your pictures?'

'Shush. Yes, it's going okay. It's just the way things have worked out. I can't tell you more than that. Sorry.'

''s all right.'

'Have you got the taxi fare?'

'Have I got taxi fare? I've been winning here, haven't I, Jude?' She leaned back to look around me. 'Cliff, this is Jude.'

Jude was lean and dark, Aboriginal. She flashed white teeth at me and laughed. 'Hi, Cliff.'

I said hello and kissed Tania's cheek. She didn't pull away and she'd barely paused in her button pressing throughout the conversation. Jude whooped as a shower of coins cascaded into her tray. 'Hey, Cliff, stick around, you're bringing me luck.'

'Quit while you're ahead.'

'He's no fun, Tania.'

I headed back to where the serious gambling was going on.

Wendy's party had moved to another table and the crowd had moved with them. I kept my distance, but the signs were she was still making waves. I worked my way around until I could get a frontal view of the man I was privately calling Shottie. He was close to 190 centimetres and a hundred kilos with long, dark hair in a short ponytail. Some flab but not much, sideburns. He moved to catch hold of a waiter, and my identification of him was confirmed; just as you can identify footballers and tennis players in action on television before you see their faces, his movement stamped him as the man I'd seen jogging down the fairway in Wollongong.

I scouted around for somewhere I could lure him to, to isolate him. The toilets wouldn't do; there were bound to be surveillance cameras. Likewise any of the doors leading to administrative areas. I wondered about the fire stairs, but they seemed to be the special concern of a security guy whose eyes never left the door. It looked as if the car park was the only possibility and there was a certain irony in that.

It was a tricky manoeuvre. I wanted him to spot me and think I hadn't noticed. But I also wanted to see exactly what he did. I thought it out and made my move. Shottie was getting bored with the roulette and was looking over towards a blackjack table where the female dealer was a redhead. The uniform of white shirt, black trousers and vest suited her creamy complexion and statuesque figure. Shottie had been drinking solidly and the redhead was getting to him in a big way. I drifted past his field of vision, timing it precisely. I mimed raising my glass and fingering the few chips in my hand, but the mirror to my right let me keep him well in sight.

He saw me and reacted by emptying his glass and bending down to mutter something to the other guy attending Wendy. I caught the conspiratorial nod and then I lost visual contact as I moved beyond the mirror. I picked it up seconds later in another reflection as I went towards the exit. Shottie was coming after me at a fast clip, but this time I was ready for him and he didn't know it. And he was drunk or close to it and I wasn't. He was younger and bigger, but I fancied my chances.

I swerved and went to the nearest cage to redeem my chips. It gave me a chance to confirm that he was on my trail. I put the notes in my wallet, took out my keys and, weaving just a little, jiggled them as I walked. I went out past the sprouting water and down the ramp leading to the escalator to the car park. I was well ahead of him, stepping off at the bottom, at a guess, just as he stepped on. I crouched behind a pillar. He came at a fair clip down the escalator and was a fraction off balance when he hit bottom. I made a fist around the keys and, with my weight moving forward, drove a right into his kidneys. The breath went out of him and he sagged. I kicked his right knee into hyper-extension and he yelled and went down hard. His head bounced on the concrete and his flailing left arm cracked against the pillar.

Pumped up, I dragged him behind the pillar and held him from behind with his right arm up behind his back. He was young, heavily muscled and strong. He resisted as much as he could but he was winded and hurting in too many places.

'Give it up,' I said close to his ear.

'Fuck you.'

I wrenched the arm and dislocated his shoulder. 'Want to try for the other one?'

'No.'

'Okay, who put you on to me with the shotgun?'

'Fuck you.'

I increased the pressure. 'What was that?'

'You'd better do the other arm,' he said through clenched teeth, 'because if I tell you anything I'm dead anyway.'

'Can't argue with that.' Keeping the good arm tightly locked, I reached inside his jacket and pulled out his wallet. His driver's licence identified him as Matthew Lonsdale with an address in Wollongong. I unshipped my mobile and dialled a number.

'I want to leave a message for Detective Inspector Farrow.'

'Can I have your name, sir?'

'No. Tell Farrow he should look for a man named Matthew Lonsdale in connection with the murder of Adam MacPherson.' I read Lonsdale's address off his licence. 'Farrow should go to that address now and he might find a sawn-off shotgun—'

Lonsdale wriggled frantically and I gave his battered arm a twist. 'At present Lonsdale is in Sydney in the company of a woman named Wendy Jones who is staying at the Novotel on Darling Harbour.'

'Sir, I request—'

'Lie there!'

'Sir?'

'Not you.'

I gave Lonsdale's knee a tap with my foot, moved away and spoke the description and registration number of Wendy's BMW into the phone in a low voice. I told the call monitor where Lonsdale was at present and cut the connection.

Lonsdale rolled onto his back and looked up at me enquiringly, his face twisted in pain and fear. I rubbed behind my ear where his shotgun had broken the skin. I showed him the spot of blood on my finger.

'Remember this morning? I'd say we were even, but you probably wouldn't agree. 'Course, I didn't have to wade through a shitty creek.'

He stared up at me, expecting a kick or worse, but I walked away.

My attack on Lonsdale might not have been the smartest move to make, but at least I'd learned something. Wendy Jones was certainly a player in whatever was going on in the Illawarra, but she wasn't the major player. Her behaviour suggested that she was out for a good time in the here and now, not a long-term planner. And Lonsdale's statement that he'd be killed if he revealed who'd hired him to heavy me carried weight. Someone, somewhere, had a lot at stake.

But my actions had put me in the firing line for who-ever that was and would also make me a target for the police. If I was going to be of any use to Elizabeth Farmer I had to stay clear of both those forces as best I could.

Smartest way was to get home, pack a bag and find a bolthole. I had a mobile phone and a laptop computer for communication and allies of a sort in Aaron De Witt and Tom Purcell, the undercover guy. If I'd jarred something loose in the Wollongong operation they might help me identify it.

I shot a quick look back at Lonsdale. He'd struggled to his feet and immediately collapsed. I took the escalator down two levels to where I'd parked the Falcon. On the way I cursed myself for not checking whether he had a mobile phone. If he had, his mate could be on the way. I roared up the ramps and got clear of the car park as fast as I could. I made the Glebe Island Bridge in good time and not too soon because I saw the blue lights and heard the sirens of cop cars heading for the casino.

I relaxed when I got clear of Darling Harbour and that was a mistake because I opted for the wrong lane and got caught in a traffic snarl on Victoria Road. A bus had hit a car and the traffic was banked up to the Rozelle turn off. Like a few other drivers, I attempted to work my way around the jam. Too many with the same idea. The traffic thickened and almost stopped. Still some movement, but so slow.

By the time I got back on track I'd lost almost half an hour and was starting to wonder how long the cops and the Wollongong interest would take to track me home. I had no choice but to get there. I needed the equipment, including the .38. I approached carefully, taking the lane behind my street first and then circling round to make a pass in front of my house. Nothing untoward. I came around again and parked a few metres away from my usual spot, which happened to be empty.

Most of the alcohol and adrenalin had drained away by this time and I was feeling edgy but under control. I left the car unlocked and strode towards the front gate, pushed it open and surged to the front door. My foot caught on something and I fell, only saving myself by grabbing at what had tripped me.

'Cliff, oh, Cliff, you must help me.'

19

Marisha Karatsky and I clutched each other, fighting for balance. She'd been sitting on the step and I'd blundered into her in the dark.

'Marisha, what the hell . . . ?'

'Don't be angry. I can explain everything. But you must help me. He's going to take her away.'

She was clinging to me with a strength I wouldn't have expected. She wore dark clothes, helping to explain why I hadn't seen her. I wasn't as much in control as I'd thought—coming down, but still in a heightened state of alertness and apprehension after what had happened at the casino, and the smell and feel of her confused me. I found myself holding her, drawing her close to me.

'Oh, Cliff . . .'

I wanted to forget all about runaway teenagers, and Swedish pimps and cops and men with shotguns, and take her inside and carry her up the stairs. I fought the feeling down.

'Marisha, it's dangerous here. There're things going on. I can't explain. I have to grab some stuff and leave.'

There was no way she was going to allow it. She gripped

my arm and her fingers bit hard. 'Together. We go together and then you can help me.'

I didn't have time to argue. With her still holding on, I made it to the door, opened it and lurched inside.

'This has to be quick,' I said. 'The police are probably on their way and other people who'll try to kill me. If you stay with me you're in the same kind of trouble.'

'I'll stay.'

'Keep out of the doorway then. I'm collecting stuff. You can go through to the next room and the kitchen and grab anything you want. Two minutes!'

I went up the stairs three at a time and into the bedroom. I collected some clothes and stuffed them in an oversized tennis bag. From the spare room the laptop went into the bag along with the Smith & Wesson from a locked drawer. I went back down and grabbed things from the bathroom. Marisha was standing in the kitchen drinking wine from a tumbler.

'We've gotta go,' I said.

She shoved the corked bottle into her big shoulder bag and followed me to the door without a word. I left lights burning, activated the alarm and closed the door.

'Have you got a car?'

She shook her head and I propelled her towards the Falcon. She slid into the seat. I slung my bag into the back and took off.

'Where are we going, Cliff?'

'I haven't worked that out yet. Just going.'

'The police are after you?'

'Not exactly. Can you keep quiet for a bit, Marisha? I have to think.'

'You tell me to be quiet when my daughter's life

is in danger. Is your other business more important than that?'

I realised that I was driving poorly and aimlessly, a sure way to be spotted by the cops who certainly had my registration number. My usual point of refuge, the Rooftop Motel in Glebe, had closed down. More redevelopment. I thought about the University Motor Inn—quiet and secluded in a one-way street, which was why it had appealed to Sallie-Anne Huckstepp and her lovers in days gone by. Bad idea. The cops would canvas motels within a few kilometres of my house as a matter of routine.

I turned onto Bridge Road, went past the old, defunct Children's Hospital, and made the turn that would take me up to Annandale and Leichhardt. I was thinking about Wesley Scott's gym on Norton Street and the flat nearby that Hank Bachelor, who'd worked for me on other cases, had recently rented. Still bad thinking. Both connections were too easily tracked. I lost concentration, almost stalled the car, and stopped outside a fast-food joint in Annandale. Marisha looked at me.

'You're hungry?'

'No, I'm conflicted. Marisha, you're an actor. Kristina's an actor. You're both very good, but I don't think I can believe anything you say. You lied to me at the beginning and you're probably lying now.'

'Who have you been talking to?'

'It doesn't matter.'

'Yes, it does.'

'A woman named Karen Bach who knew your daughter at school . . . and after.'

'I don't know her. You believe her?'

'I don't know what to believe and I don't think I care.'

She put her hand on my thigh. 'You cared when we made love.'

'I think you were using me. I think that's what you do. What you're doing now.'

She moved her hand away and pushed back against the seat, banging her head against the headrest. 'All right. All right. Let the poor little junkie, hooker bitch die. What does it matter? And let her randy, reffo mother go mad. Who cares?'

Despite all the pressure and tension, I burst out laughing. 'Marisha, they're the worst lines I've ever heard spoken by a real live person. You must have translated them from some Mexican movie.'

She went rigid and for a second I thought she was going to attack me; then she shook her tangle of hair and let out a long, slow breath. A throaty chuckle followed.

'Yes, I went too far there.'

'I was right, then. This is all a game?'

She sighed, pulled the wine bottle from her bag, uncorked it and took a swig. 'Not very ladylike, but then, I'm not a lady.'

I took the bottle and had a drink. 'And I'm not a gentleman. Tell me what's going on or you're out of this car right now.'

'I knew Kristina would be with Stefan but I didn't know where. I thought you might find them both.'

'Sorry to disappoint you. Why did you disappear?'

'You won't believe me.'

'Try me.'

'Kristina phoned me and asked to meet. She insisted that I come alone. She specifically said not to tell you or bring you and then she gave me . . . what is it? The runaround.'

'Meaning?'

'Oh, I know you won't believe this, but it's true. As in the movies. I was to go to a place and phone her. Then to another. I suppose they were watching me all the time. I got lost. I was frightened. It was terrible, Cliff.'

'And what was the upshot?'

'What's that word you used—conflicted? I was. I'm guessing that this Karen Bach is another prostitute and she told you I used Kristina to lure Stefan. More lies from Kristina. It's not true. It was all much more complicated than that.'

I could get my head around that, just. 'You didn't answer the question.'

'Yes, all right. I met her. I didn't really recognise her. She was so different. So . . . It doesn't matter now. She has a passport. Stefan has taken her to New Zealand.'

'Marisha, she's fifteen!'

'No. She turned sixteen. Yesterday.'

A fine rain had started to fall as we were speaking and Marisha was sobbing quietly. I watched the windscreen fog up from our breath and body heat and become opaque as the rain fell, more insistently now. On the one hand, I wanted to analyse and evaluate what she'd told me; on the other, I just wanted to believe her. The doubt produced another question.

'So why did you come to my place tonight and . . . put on that act?'

'You don't know?'

'I know fuck-all, and that least of anything.'

The sobbing slowed, then stopped. 'I wanted to be with you.'

I grunted and shook my head.

'Cliff, didn't it mean anything?'

'It did, and then it didn't.'

'Because of what Karen Bach told you?'

'I suppose so. I don't know.'

'I've told you the truth.'

'Give me the bottle.'

She handed it over and I drained it, hoping to get some kind of a charge. Didn't happen. 'Marisha, your daughter, you say, has gone off to another country with a paedophile pimp. And you . . .'

She turned her face towards me. It was wan under its olive tint, tear-stained and makeup streaked, but there was life and hope in her huge dark eyes. 'She told me she didn't hate me. She said she loved me. She said she'd write and phone and that she'd see me again soon. My daughter.'

If she had gone on about wanting me, I might have pushed her out into the rain. But now I wanted strongly to believe her. She had the look I'd seen before—when I'd located a runaway and brought him or her home. The hopelessness, displayed in the speech and body language of the parents, vanished in an instant on the doorstep and their world was back as something manageable, or almost, at least for now.

'That's good,' I said.

We sat quietly for a time while the rain beat on the car roof. I realised that, for all the deception and doubt and much of it not dispelled, I was glad she was there.

'So,' she said, 'you know I am what is called a drama queen.'

I grinned. 'You are indeed.'

'Tell me why you are running away from your house.'

'It's complicated. It's this other business I've been dealing with. I have to stay out of sight and try to work out what to do next. The police know where I live, so do the bad guys, probably. They know this car.'

'Do they know of your connection to me?'

'No.'

'You could do your thinking at my place.'

I was about to say no as a matter of instinct—emotional complication was the last thing I needed—when my mobile rang. I made an apologetic gesture to Marisha and answered it, expecting the cops or worse.

'Hardy.'

'Where is she?'

'Dr Farmer, I'm sorry. I was going to call you. It's been a hell of a night. I had to leave Tania at the casino. She had plenty of money to get home. Isn't she—?'

'No, she fucking isn't. Who did you leave her with?'

'What?'

'I'm speaking English, aren't I? You're not telling me you left her standing at a roulette wheel with a pile of chips in her hand.'

'No. She was playing the poker machines and she'd struck up a conversation—'

'With a woman?'

'Yes, an Aboriginal woman named—'

'I don't want to know her fucking name. Aboriginal. Jesus. Well, thank you very much.'

She cut the connection and I stared blankly at the phone.

'Dr Farmer,' Marisha said. 'Your other client?'

'Right.'

'An angry man?'

'An angry woman.'

'That's worse. Come on, Cliff. It's a terrible night. You look troubled and you don't know what to do next. Have you got a better offer?'

20

Marisha's apartment was warm and welcoming. We went to bed and made love, not with the passion of the previous occasion, but looking for and finding mutual comfort. I slept. My mobile rang a couple of times and sometime in the night I crawled out of bed to switch it off.

'That might be important,' Marisha said.

I slid back into the rough, deep red cotton sheets, pulled her towards me and wrapped myself around her small body. 'All the more reason to ignore it. I can't deal with anything important right now.'

She stiffened momentarily, then relaxed. 'I understand.'

I dug my hand into her mass of hair and put my face down to inhale its smell. 'Do you?' I said. 'I wish I did.'

'You're making no sense. Go back to sleep.'

But, strangely, I wasn't tired anymore. I lay with my arms around her, staring up at the ceiling. A certain amount of street or moonlight or both filtered into the room through the matchstick blinds. I began to run over the various strands of the Farmer case in my mind and found myself able to separate them out and look at each with some clarity. Minutes slipped by as I did the sort of analysis

I could usually best manage when charged up with caffeine or alcohol. Without those stimulants I was still physically worn but mentally alert. Good sex can have strange effects. Marisha muttered and pulled away from me. I let her go.

There was something big stirring in the Illawarra. Big enough to warrant two deaths already—Frederick Farmer and Adam MacPherson—and an attempted third, mine. The Wombarra land owned by Sue Holland and Elizabeth Farmer was somehow at the centre of it. Outlaw bikies were involved and, more than likely, some of the local police. I couldn't put Barton's behaviour down to incompetence or antagonism. Behind it all was some big contractor paying out big money—a sizeable chunk to Wendy Jones—tied in, probably, to the acquisition of Sue Holland's land. Was Elizabeth Farmer's land still targeted?

My sources of information were De Witt, Purcell and possibly Farrow. Marisha was right. I couldn't afford to be out of touch. I switched on the mobile. The calls had been from Farrow first and then Elizabeth Farmer. I didn't want to talk to Farrow just yet and whether Tania had come home or not, there was nothing I could do about it.

Marisha was deeply asleep. I dressed quietly and went back to where I'd left my bag. I plugged in the laptop and booted it up. The solitary message was from Purcell. It read: *Hardy, I've got a line on what's happening down here. If you want in on it, meet me at the pub just up from that crummy motel you were in—tomorrow at 10.00. Like before, wipe this.*

I deleted the message and cleared the trash. Annoying not to be able to reply, ask for more detail, but it was a different Hotmail address from the one before and my guess was that he used them once only. I shut the computer down and leaned back in the chair to think. I was confused. I couldn't see why Purcell would want me to be in on anything, let alone guess what it might be. And he couldn't have known when he sent the message, at 9.16 pm, that the events of the night would make me a hot property in the Illawarra.

Every cautious instinct said stay away. Every curious instinct, backed up by professional pride, said go there. No contest. I'd left my watch by the bed and didn't know the time. The digits on Marisha's stove and microwave blinked on double zeros and I knew what that meant. She hadn't reset them after a power failure. Not unknown at my place. It made me feel friendly towards her as I crouched down by the bed to retrieve the watch. It scraped harshly on the polished floor but she didn't stir. I slipped the watch on and stood, looking down at her. Her dark hair was spread out on the red pillow and one hand was cocked up near her mouth as if she was speaking on a phone. I realised that I had no idea what I thought about her.

It was five forty-five, still dark and a blanket of quiet and stillness hung over this part of Sydney. I could get on the road, stop for breakfast and a shave somewhere along the way and be in the Illawarra early enough to consider exactly what to do. Except that . . . Marisha's bag sat on the floor, gaping open. I dug into it, feeling around, and came up with a set of keys. The car keys were attached to an NRMA tag carrying the make and registration number. A Hyundai. I detached the car keys and pocketed them. I went into her work room and found a pad and paper. The note I left told her I'd borrowed her car and would get it back as soon as possible. I said I'd left my car keys but she wasn't to use the Falcon except in an emergency because the police would be looking for it. I felt I owed her that much at least.

. . .

The Hyundai didn't have a lot of power but it handled well and I made good time south as daylight dawned. I'd only had a couple of hours sleep but I felt almost fully charged. I caught an early news service on the radio—the usual stuff, the government under attack for lying and lying some more in response. A major marijuana haul up north had the police puffing out their chests. The weather was going to be fine along the coast and the bright, slightly cloud-streaked sky told me the same.

I stopped at a servo in Heathcote, topped up the tank and went into the restaurant. I ordered coffee and toast and had a quick wash and shave. The coffee was surprisingly good and the toast was unsurprisingly limp and soggy but I lingered over it anyway, trying to work out my next moves. I flicked through a local paper lying around and found an article on the closure of the coast road. The state government had allotted forty million dollars to fix it and the project would take two and a half years to complete. Locals were protesting that there were more accidents on the freeway in fog than on the coast road from falling rocks. I wondered about the crack. I decided it was a good omen.

It was the best time of the day to come down the Bulli Pass. The sun was above the horizon, but not by much, and a mist was lifting off the water and the land. The townships to north and south were spread out before me with the sand and the sea as an immense backdrop punctuated here and there by Norfolk Island pines.

I pegged Sue Holland as an early riser and I was right. When I'd steered the little car down the rutted track and pulled up in front of her cottage there was smoke rising from her chimney and Fred the old dog was moving freely as if he'd been up and about for a while. He barked, but he had my scent memory-logged, and he didn't give me any trouble. Sue Holland came around from the back with a steaming cup in her hand. She had on a long, loose sweater over red flannel pyjamas, fluffy slippers.

'Jesus Christ,' she said. 'What d'you want?'

There, under the escarpment, the temperature was low. I rubbed my hands together. 'Beautiful morning, isn't it? How can you bear to leave?'

Her aggression dropped away and a shadow of sadness passed across her face. She raised the cup to her mouth and took a long sip. 'Just what I need,' she said. 'Someone to bore it up me.'

'I don't want to give you a bad time, Sue. And I'm grateful for what you told Elizabeth to pass on to me. Very useful. But I need a bit more. Can we go inside? It's a bit parky.'

'What? Oh, cold. I haven't heard that expression in a while.'

'I've got a few, like taters. No idea where they come from. My grandma used to say she was "starved with the cold".'

'The old Hardy blather and bullshit. Okay, come in. I can give you a cup of coffee, but I don't know what more I can tell you.'

I gave Fred a pat and followed her back to the rear of the cottage and into the kitchen. It was warm and smelled of coffee and tobacco. Sue drained her cup and refilled it from the pot on the combustion stove. She filled a mug for me and put it on the table. Then she picked up the makings in a clear plastic pouch and rolled a cigarette. She lit it with a disposable lighter, puffed smoke and slumped down into a chair.

'I started again. Seven years off, and I'm back into it. Chop chop. At least it's cheap.'

I shrugged. 'Might be healthier, too. I don't suppose you'll tell me how much the offer is?'

'No. High six figures, very high.'

'Nice. Especially as they say prices around here might drop depending on the effect of the road closure. Care to name the buyer?'

'How dumb do I look, Cliffo?'

The coffee was about five times as good as the last one. 'Not very.'

'I did a bit of an internet search. It's a maze. But I'll tell you what. The deposit cheque cleared and they're not interested in a building inspection or a pest report or any of that shit.'

'Dream run.'

'Fuck you.'

'Why did you go up there and tell Elizabeth about the sale?'

She took a deep drag, sucked the smoke in and let it out slowly. The technique was coming back to her fast. 'Shit. I had some crazy idea I might . . . You said you didn't know whether she had anyone or not. Just a chance. Then I saw how happy she was . . . Did Liz tell you anything about me?'

'No. Yes, she said you'd know the sound of a motorbike if you heard it.'

'You bet. I was a dropout bikie chick. Chains, tatts, speed, dope, the works. Then I met her and everything changed. I got educated and employed and then I lost her.

I got a little nest egg, like I told you, and bought this place. And now I've got a big one and I don't give a fuck where it comes from.'

I finished the coffee while she was talking and put the cup quietly down on the table as a gesture of acceptance. 'Fair enough. Just one more question. The settlement is when?'

She took a drag on the cigarette and flicked the ash on the floor. 'In record time, baby,' she said.

I rejoined the coast road at Coledale and stayed on it until Fairy Meadow where I picked up the freeway to Nowra, bypassing the city. I took the turnoff and was passing the Warrawong motel shortly after nine o'clock. Time to kill. I drove down towards the Port Kembla steelworks and got as close as I could to the port itself. The harbour was basic-ally artificial, formed by two long breakwaters. A couple of container ships were berthed at the jetties and there were some fishing boats and leisure craft. Seagulls squatted on the boat masts and the rusty machinery on the docks. As I watched, a couple of pelicans flew over from the direction of the lake and settled on the water. Peaceful scene.

I drove back the way I'd come and spotted Purcell's old Land Cruiser in the hotel car park. The pub had just opened and there were a few early drinkers' cars parked but none close to the Land Cruiser. I drove in and parked about twenty metres away. I could see Purcell behind the wheel and I decided to let him make the first move. If he wanted to meet in the bar, well and good. If he wanted a fresh air conference that was okay by me as well. I sat for five minutes and he didn't move. I got out of the little car and stretched. An alert type like Purcell would certainly see me and make his move.

Nothing happened. A couple of cars pulled in and parked, still a fair distance away. The sun was high now and I stripped off my jacket and slung it inside the car. I walked towards the Land Cruiser and felt a tingle in my spine as I got closer. I was well within his field of vision now and he still hadn't moved. I reached the vehicle on the driver's side. The window was down. Purcell was strapped into place by his seatbelt and his head was thrown back. The hair at his temple was matted with blood. His eyes were open but he wasn't seeing anything and never would again.

21

I didn't stay close to the Land Cruiser for one second more than I needed to. And I didn't back away. Nothing looks more suspicious than backing. I walked around the front of the car as if I was interested in its age and condition and then veered away towards the pub. The low calibre execution of Purcell was a professional job, carried out within the last hour and possibly within minutes of my arrival in the car park. Presumably Purcell had got there early and the killer had followed him and decided it would be as good a time and place as any. If I'd shown up maybe he would have put the matter off, or maybe he would have decided to make it two for the price of one.

I've seen a lot of death but it never fails to register in some part of the brain as a shock. The way you do, I'd built up a picture of how my meeting with Purcell might go. He'd been alive in my imagination and in a way he still was, but now he wasn't alive in reality and it took a bit of adjusting to. I went into the bar and ordered a scotch and a middy. No eyebrows raised. There are some serious drinkers in the Illawarra. I downed the scotch and took the beer out the side door to a verandah that gave me a view of the car park.

The early crowd was evidently in place because no more cars came in. The dirty old 4WD still stood, semi-isolated.

I put the beer down on the verandah rail, took my mobile from my pants pocket and called Farrow.

'Hardy.' His voice was an angry rasp. 'Where the fuck are you? What was all that shit last night?'

'Did you find Wendy and her pals?'

'No.'

'Did you search Lonsdale's place?'

'No comment. What're you playing at?'

I couldn't hang around much longer. Someone was bound to spot Purcell. I tossed up whether or not to tell Farrow about it. I decided. I told him where he'd find the body of a man I thought to be an undercover policeman.

'Stay there,' he said.

'Yeah, I'll do that so you can take me in and keep me on a chair for the rest of the day and probably longer.'

'Stay there.'

'No chance, and I'll give you this for free—I don't think every single one of your colleagues is playing on your team.'

'What the hell do you mean?'

I cut the connection and drained the beer. The trick to walking as if you're unconcerned isn't to whistle or put your hands in your pockets. It's a matter of minimal upper body movement and pace and line. I reached the Hyundai, unlocked it, got in and drove out of the car park without glancing at the Land Cruiser, although I gave Purcell a silent salutation as I went past.

I headed back to Wollongong. Two police cars going full pelt with sirens screaming shot by as I drove at a sedate pace. I had very little idea what to do next, particularly as I wasn't even sure I had a client after last night's doings. I parked behind the railway station and called Elizabeth Farmer. No reply at home; voicemail at the university. I swore several times, then the phone rang.

'Cliff, this is Tania Vronsky. I just missed your call.'

'I was checking to see if Elizabeth was still employing me.'

'Why wouldn't she be?'

I told her about the phone call from Elizabeth and she laughed. 'Oh, she's like that. Jealous as hell. No, I didn't get off with Jude. She was much more pissed than me by the time we finished playing. I got her home and then got back myself, very late. All's well. How're things working out for you?'

'I don't know. When you next see Elizabeth tell her I'm still on it and sort of making progress, but the cops might be calling on her.'

'How exciting. Fact is, Cliff, this business has given our relationship quite a boost. What does she tell them?'

'The truth,' I said.

I was sitting there indecisively when I became aware of someone standing by the passenger window. DS Barton of Bellambi rapped on the glass with his pistol, gesturing for me to open that door and the one behind me. He'd have no trouble shooting me through the glass and no compunction either, from the look of him. I opened the doors. A man slid in to the back seat as Barton got in beside me. I took a quick look in the rear vision mirror. Didn't know him, but everything about him said cop.

'You look surprised, Hardy.'

'I am.'

'Because you're not in your car?'

'Yes.'

He held the pistol low, out of sight. 'Can't figure it out?'

'No.'

'Your girlfriend reported it stolen. You became a hot item after that performance last night. Wasn't too hard to pick you up.'

I let out a long slow breath. Marisha Karatsky was certainly full of surprises. I was careful to keep my hands in sight on the wheel. Not that it'd make much difference. If Barton wanted to shoot me he could. It was between trains and there was no one much about and it was a fair bet that either I'd have a gun he could use to make it look okay or he'd have a throw-down to hand. It'd been done before.

'So what's this about?' I said.

'I thought you were smart enough to take a hint that you weren't wanted down here.'

'I'm a little slow sometimes.'

'That can be just as fatal as speed. Start the car and go where I tell you.'

'Suppose I don't?'

'Then you get a clout on the head from behind and you go where we're going anyway.'

I started the engine. 'Are you going to let me know what this's about?'

'I don't think so. Just shut up and do as you're told. Put your seatbelt on and no heroics.'

For the second time, and too close to the first, I felt gun metal behind my ear. Different deal this time—two to contend with and them official and probably experienced at this sort of work. Even if I contrived some kind of crash, I'd be too dead to take any advantage. I had nothing to bargain with, nothing to offer, no way to threaten. I drove like an automaton, obeying Barton's instructions because there seemed nothing else to do. I was beginning to get the blank-to-everything-around-me feeling, as if I was dead already.

'Scared, Hardy?'

Barton was breaking his own rules but I couldn't see much hope in that. If he was a little nervous all that was likely to happen was that he wouldn't do a clean job.

'I wouldn't give you the satisfaction.'

'Oh, job satisfaction? I've got plenty of that.'

'Nice hit on the undercover guy. Who's handy with the .22—you or the silent one in the back?'

'Not something for you to worry about.'

'You might worry about who he's told what to.'

'Oh, I know all that. And I know he's told you bugger-all.'

I chewed that over just to have something else to think about. If what Barton said was true, Purcell's operation was compromised somehow. Too bad. He'd seemed good at what he did.

I realised that we were heading for the waste area where the bikies held their races and drug supermarket. I hadn't taken in much about it on my last visit because my night vision isn't all that flash. Seemed like a good place for what this pair had in mind—quiet when not noisy, out of the way, dirty, and with lots of leather and denim watch-dogs. All the traffic had dropped away as we'd left the main roads and now we were on a rough, narrow strip of bitumen that was rotting and falling in at the sides. It twisted and turned as it went through patches of scrub and saltwater flats—not the best scenery for your last look at the world.

A couple of buildings I hadn't noticed before were scattered around the area—sheds mostly, a couple of shipping containers, a sagging prefab garage. Barton directed me to drive over close to the garage which meant going around a high pile of aggregate being readied for laying. I considered trying to run the car up its side to get it to roll and then take my chances but with two guns on me the chances weren't worth the effort.

I pulled up by the garage. 'Now what?'

'Out carefully, hands behind.'

I stepped out and Barton's mate neatly handcuffed me.

'Right,' Barton said. 'Let's get this over with. Get the bobcat, Jake.'

Jake slid open the garage doors. I heard an engine start up and the bobcat lurched out into the sunlight. It stalled. Jake swore and got the motor running again at high, noisy revs. Another stall and he repeated the procedure.

'Has he got a licence for that thing?' I said.

'Brave face. On your knees, Hardy.'

'No chance.' I turned and walked away from him. There was nowhere to go and I knew I couldn't outrun him with my hands pinioned, but he was going to have to chase me and shoot me and when he did I was going to be on my feet.

'Stop!'

I didn't.

I heard the shot and for an instant I thought he'd missed and waited for the next. Then three shots followed in quick succession and I hit the dirt, fast and hard. Without hands to protect my fall I landed on my face, bounced and skidded and my eyes and mouth filled with dirt. I lay still, spluttering and coughing and blinking. I rolled onto my side and screwed around to look back. The bobcat was where it had stopped and its motor was still running but Jake wasn't at the controls. He was pushed back against it with his hands held high. A figure writhed on the ground, yelling obscenities and throwing up little puffs of dust.

I pulled myself up, tripped and fell and got up again. My eyes were streaming but my vision was clearing. A man who I could now see was in uniform jerked Jake's hands down and cuffed him. The other man stood near the figure on the ground talking into his mobile phone. He started walking towards me, still talking, and I could see that he held a pistol in his hand. He stopped talking and closed the phone. I backed off a few steps, not knowing what to think.

He swung around and shouted, 'Shut that fuckin' thing off!'

The motor died and the area became quiet. The man who'd issued the order reached behind him and holstered his pistol. He walked towards me with his hands open in a benign gesture. I recognised Inspector Ian Farrow from Wollongong and realised that I was still alive and likely to remain so.

Farrow stopped a metre away. 'Hardy,' he said. 'You are one lucky, lucky bastard.'

22

Sirens wailed and an ambulance and more police cars arrived but I was oblivious to most of it. They uncuffed me, sat me down in the back of a car with the door open and gave me a damp towel. I wiped at my eyes and mouth and felt the sting of fresh cuts and the dull ache of developing bruises. My face was pretty battered, my knees were sore and my clothes were a mess. I didn't care. I was alive. After a while I looked around and cracked a smile although it hurt my face. A flock of seagulls was perched on top of the bobcat that had been brought out to plough me under.

The ambulance and one of the cop cars sped off and Farrow had the time to come over and talk to me. I thanked him before he could say anything.

'Thank *you*,' he said.

'Why's that?'

'Let's get you back to the station and I'll fill you in. You're all right, aren't you? Nothing broken?'

'Never better, considering.'

'Right. I'll get one of our blokes to drive your car. Or rather, Ms Karatsky's car.'

One of the cops started up the bobcat and the seagulls flew away. I watched them as they headed off towards the coast. I fastened the seatbelt and leaned back prepared to enjoy the ride. With my eyes clearing and my mouth starting not to taste like the inside of a football boot, I was beginning to think about what I was working on and how what I'd just been through bore on it. I decided to give it up until I'd heard from Farrow. I closed my eyes and found myself humming 'A Whiter Shade of Pale'. The cop sitting next to me gave me an odd look and I grinned at him. It still hurt to smile, but not as much.

'We've known Clive Barton and some of his boys, like Jacob Henderson, were dirty for a while,' Farrow said. 'They've been under surveillance. Drugs mostly, import and manu-facture, but also facilitating armed hold-ups and maybe the odd hit.'

We were sitting in Farrow's office in the Wollongong Police HQ. I'd had a decent wash and gargle and had a mug of coffee in my hand. My cuts and abrasions and bruises weren't hurting too badly thanks to a couple of Panadeine Fortes.

'But Clive was very careful and we had nothing solid, so when they picked you up and had you lined up for an execution, it gave us the opportunity to arrest them. And that'll allow us to put some pressure on the bunch. See who'll squeal on who.'

Elizabeth Farmer would have said 'whom' but I wasn't going to quibble. Farrow went on to say he'd monitored Marisha's report of the stolen Hyundai and when the team tailing Barton and Henderson saw that they had picked me up they knew they had something and went into action.

'I didn't see anyone tailing me and believe me I was looking,' I said.

'We were well back. We were only able to get close when Jake started fucking around with that bobcat. Bought you some time. Anyway, that's what I meant when I thanked you.'

'Any time. Do you think Barton had anything to do with Purcell's death?'

'It's possible. One of his other cronies is a target shooter. Be hard to prove though.'

'So I'll have to testify when they go up for abduction and attempted murder?'

Farrow remained silent.

'Won't I?'

'That'll depend on how it works out. What else gets admitted to. Who else gets given up. You know how it works.'

'Sure, so now that we're pals, you can tell me whether you got hold of Wendy Jones and Lonsdale and the other one.'

Farrow shook his head. 'No sign of them. Checked out of the Novotel and vanished.'

'What about Lonsdale's shottie?'

Farrow had to consider that one. Eventually he nodded. 'Found a sawn-off shotgun in his panniers. We want him.'

'Wendy's a part of this Farmer thing I told you about. She's got something to do with whoever's interested in that land. Barton didn't bother properly investigating the fire that killed my client's father. He's tied to it as well.'

I talked on for a bit, describing the first time I'd been taken for a ride, and Farrow made some notes. 'We'll ask him about it and I'll let you know if we get anything.'

'You know there's something big being planned down here,' I said. 'I put some pressure on that Lonsdale character to tell me who'd ordered me killed but he said he'd be dead himself if he talked. He meant it.'

Farrow shrugged. 'Could've meant Clive.'

'I don't think so.'

'Why not?'

'Just a feeling. Barton strikes me more as senior management than a CEO type. And there's some big seed money around.'

I told him about the inflated price paid for Sue Holland's land, even considering the high prices in the area, and the possibility that Wendy Jones was involved in the fire that killed Frederick Farmer. As soon as I said it, it struck me that the suspicions about Farmer's death had firmed up to something like a fact and I reacted sharply, almost spilling my coffee.

'What?' Farrow said.

'I thought Farmer's death was an accident—the fire was just an attempt to shift him, but what if he'd sussed out why his land was wanted and he was deliberately killed to shut him up.'

'That's very speculative.'

'Speculation is my middle name. If it's right it puts Wendy in the frame for murder. What's being done on that score?'

'Everything possible and you stay out of it. After what's happened recently I don't imagine you want to tangle with a bunch of speed freak bikies.'

'No, but it's not the bikies I'm concerned about, it's Wendy's connection with the string puller. You must have candidates.'

'Oh, there're candidates, but again, keep clear.'

'I was hired to find out what happened to my client's dad and why.'

'Well, you've got a good theory. Sell her that.'

I put the coffee mug on his desk and looked at him.

'Sorry,' he said, 'but it's a police matter. We'll keep you informed of course.'

'Okay.' I got to my feet and Farrow stood up too.

'If you'd stuck around the way you should've when you found Purcell, this wouldn't have happened to you.'

'And you wouldn't have got the handle on Barton.'

'True.' Farrow smiled. 'And then there's the little matter of the car you stole.'

'Borrowed, and I left her a note.'

'Doesn't seem to have mattered. Well, I'll leave you to sort that out.' He reached into his pocket and handed me the keys. 'Car's out front. Watch out for yourself, Hardy.'

We shook hands and I went out. I couldn't say that I felt safe. I didn't know how far Barton's influence spread in the Illawarra force or what reprisals might be taken. He and Henderson wouldn't have risked driving around in the Hyundai so they must have had someone standing by to dispose of it and someone to pick them up. Farrow had spoken of another rotten apple, the target shooter, but there could be more.

I flinched when a shadow slanted across in front of me on the steps of the police building.

'Take it easy, Hardy. It's me, De Witt.'

He was there in his long, lanky, relaxed way, the first civilian I'd seen in quite some time and I was glad to see him. 'Jesus, you gave me a fright.'

'Not surprised. I've just been hearing what fun and

games you've been having. I can't write about it because it's all sub judice, but when the time comes . . .'

'Like I told you, you've got the story.'

He looked me up and down and I remembered the state of my clothes. 'You've been earning your money,' he said.

What money? I thought. I'd seen bloody little of it for the knocks I'd been taking.

'I've got things to tell you,' De Witt said. 'I imagine you'd be ready for a drink.'

I looked at my watch. It was almost three o'clock and I'd had nothing to eat since early morning and nothing to drink but coffee since then. 'I could do with a few drinks and a feed.'

We went to a restaurant where I used the toilet to put on a clean shirt and pants from my bag. I ordered a steak and a bottle of red wine. De Witt had fish and mineral water. He wanted to know about the morning's events and I filled him in off the record, for now. I was able to concentrate on my food and drink because De Witt had to get up frequently to go outside and smoke. Made me glad I didn't. I was forking in the last of my chips when he got around to giving me his news.

'I turned up something interesting on your Matilda Sharpe-Tarleton.'

'Yeah?'

'Seems she's got an interest in a company called Kembla Holdings. That is to say, her real estate firm does.'

'And what does Kembla Holdings do?'

'Hard to say, but a man named Larry Buckingham is not at arm's length from it.'

'So?'

'You haven't heard of Larry Buckingham?'

'Come on, Aaron, I haven't heard of lots of people. Who is he?'

'Well, he's a few things, past and present. Nowadays a highly successful publican. Spend any time down here and you're likely to drink in one of his many establishments. Owns a few places in Sydney as well. One-time footballer, charged with but not convicted of supplying amphetamines to players and others. Bit of a bikie in his time . . . and ex-lover of Wendy Jones.'

23

De Witt had asked around but couldn't get a line on what might be planned for the Wombarra acres.

'I hope your enquiries were discreet,' I said. 'I've got an idea that finding that out was what got Frederick Farmer killed.'

'Very discreet. Always. Anything solid?'

'Just a feeling, but it fits. It looks as if the two goes at knocking me off were because they thought I'd find it out, or already had. I haven't.'

'But you're going to try.'

'Yeah. I'm getting interested in this Sydney connection. Might be worth paying Matilda a visit and bringing her up to date with things. Might panic her. Say she knows Wendy and say I tell her how close Wendy is to a shotgun killing.'

'Is she?'

'Could be. Farrow found the shotgun that could've killed MacPherson. Who knows where Wendy fits in? But it wouldn't hurt to try it on Matilda for size. No word about Wendy down here, is there? The cops don't know where she is.'

De Witt drained his mineral water and shook his head. 'Nothing.'

'She could be in Sydney still. No one better placed to hide people than a real estate agent.'

'You're reaching.'

'True. Can you give me a list of the places in Sydney this Buckingham character owns?'

'Sure. I'll email it. So you're heading back to the smoke?'

'Have to. A matter of a stolen car to sort out.'

De Witt looked blank.

'Don't worry. It's a sideshow. I'll get this, or rather my client will.'

I'd drunk half of the bottle; I got the cork back and took the rest with me. I went to the toilet again and examined my face. The bruises were coming along nicely and the scratches were scabbing up. Quick healers, the Hardys.

The Falcon was where I'd left it close to Marisha's building. I pulled the Hyundai, which hadn't suffered any damage beyond wear and tear on the tyres and picking up a lot of dust, into one of the parking slots. I went to her door and rang the bell. I had the keys dangling from my index finger. The door opened and she looked at me as if I was wearing a fright mask. She retreated a step.

'Cliff. Oh, Cliff, I'm so sorry.'

'What for?'

'For reporting the car stolen. I didn't see your note and when the car wasn't there I got angry.'

'I left the note in plain view.'

'It fell down. I found it later and tried to . . . withdraw the report, but . . .'

'You didn't see my car in the street and think about it?'

'No, oh God, don't look so fierce.'

Was she acting again? I just couldn't tell. I stuck my finger out so she could take the keys but she wasn't looking at it.

'Your face! What's happened to your face? Is it my fault? Did the police . . . ?'

She had the knack. The things she said and the way she said them made me laugh. I leaned against the doorway clumsily and dropped the keys. I grunted as I bent to pick them up, something I'd pledged not to do. 'Yes,' I said. 'One cop tried to kill me and another saved my life.'

Her hands went up to her hair in a gesture that lifted her small breasts under the T-shirt and emphasised her slimness and flexibility. 'Jesus. Was this because I reported it?'

'Yes and no. They would have found me anyway, sooner or later. Can I come in?'

'Of course.' She reached for my hands and I let her pull me inside. There was a smell of incense in the apartment and I could hear some kind of classical music playing softly. Also voices speaking a foreign language. She saw me noticing and shook her head. 'I haven't got visitors. I'm working on a film translation.'

'What language?'

'Russian.'

'Lucky it isn't Arabic, you'd have ASIO after you.'

She stared at me and then the strain and doubt fell away from her face as she smiled. 'A joke. You are beaten up again and still joking. Are we going to make love again?'

'If I can,' I said.

. . .

'So, how is what you call your other matter going?'

We'd made love, but my doubts about her story and my reluctance to question her further hadn't helped. I'd slept while Marisha worked and now we were sitting over glasses of wine before deciding what to do about an evening meal. A long, hot shower had eased my aches and pains but my face still looked as if I'd played eighty minutes of State of Origin. I remembered being clobbered by a runaway surfboard once, and my face felt a bit like it had then. It hurt to frown and to laugh and I'd chipped a tooth. To my tongue it felt like a serrated edge but Marisha said she couldn't see it. I'd put off thinking about the Farmer case, but the respite was temporary.

'It's taking some sort of shape,' I said. 'But there's a fair way to go.'

'So you'll be running off again soon?'

I nodded.

'Will it be dangerous? As dangerous as it has been up to now?'

'I hope not. If I can find out how things tie together that should satisfy my client. Then it'll be a matter for the police.'

'Who is he, your client?'

'She. An academic at Sydney University.'

'Beautiful?'

'Handsome.'

'Sexy?'

'A lesbian.'

She laughed and drew closer to me on the couch. 'I didn't pay you for finding Kristina.'

'I found her but I didn't catch her. You don't have to pay me.'

'She phoned me as she said she would.'

'How's she going to manage with that bastard of a pimp?'

'I think she'll manage.'

I remembered how she'd tricked me into taking her to Paddington and how she'd coped with that situation and I thought that perhaps Marisha was right—if the story was true. My mind switched to Wendy Jones and Matilda and Larry Buckingham.

'You've gone away already,' Marisha said.

I shook my head and was pleased to feel no pain. 'Not yet.'

I brought Elizabeth Farmer up to date by telephoning her in the morning. I omitted the rough stuff but let her know there were two more possible victims of a conspiracy behind her father's death.

'And you think Dad got wind of it?'

'It's a possibility. Trouble is, it's all tissue thin. Matilda's got some sort of connection to this Kembla Holdings mob that has a dodgy smell to it. If they're involved in the purchase of Sue Holland's land it would all firm up a bit, but I don't know if it's possible to tease that out.'

'Why not?'

'Sue said she got the offer through a solicitor and tried to track back to the source of the money but didn't get very far.'

A disparaging noise came over the line. 'One, she'd be a rank amateur at that sort of thing and, two, she has an interest in not knowing.'

'I suppose that's true.'

'Now my Tania works for this massive accounting firm that's got databases and all that stuff. Maybe she could see if there's a connection between . . . what was it?'

'Kembla Holdings. Everything all right on that front, is it?'

'Yes. Kembla Holdings and the solicitor. What's his name?'

'I don't know. You'd have to ask Sue, and along the lines of what you said before, she probably won't tell you.'

'I'll spin her a story. She'll tell me. So what are you going to do, Cliff?'

'I'd like to find Wendy Jones and her pals, and I'm wondering if you're in any danger.'

'I can take care of myself, and if Matilda's behind all this she knows that I don't have a clue about it.'

'She might know—through the bent cops—that I was hired by you.'

'You said he was in custody, that policeman.'

'That's right.'

'I should pay you some money,' she said.

'It wouldn't hurt. I'll email you an account.'

We left it there. Mention of email prompted me to boot up the laptop. De Witt had listed three hotels—one in Marrickville, one in Erskineville and one in Balmain—owned by Larry Buckingham. Buckingham had played for Balmain so it was natural that his property would be in the inner west. I didn't remember him, but I've never followed League all that closely. It was a place to start. I closed up the computer and went into the room where Marisha was working.

'I have to go.'

She didn't turn around from the screen. 'Okay. Bye.'

'Something wrong?'

'No. Just me not being clingy.'

'I'll ring you, Marisha, but I don't know when.'

She swivelled the chair around to face me. She was wearing white silk pyjamas with most of the buttons undone. I could see the tops of her breasts with a thin gold chain dropping down between them. She blew me a kiss and went back to work.

A quick look told me that the Marrickville pub wasn't a goer because it was immediately across the road from the police station. The Erskineville place was more a wine bar than a pub. The upper level was occupied by offices of some sort; there was no easy parking and no easy getaway routes. It was mid-morning on a warm day so I had a drink there anyway. Plenty of football photos about. When the barman brought my beer I asked him if Larry Buckingham was in any of the photos.

'Sure,' he said. 'There he is. And there.'

The first photo was of a player running with the ball under his arm and fending off an opponent. His face was a grimace of determination and aggression and it was hard to tell from the picture what he'd look like off the field. The group photo of the team sometime in the eighties showed him to be big, dark and handsome with a face still relatively undamaged. He had muscles everywhere they were needed but there was a look about his build that suggested he would put on weight when he stopped training. But then, don't we all?

I drove to Balmain and found the pub, more or less on the border of Rozelle, a few blocks down from Darling

Street towards the water. The Soldiers Arms was shut up tight with that sad look a pub gets when it goes out of business. But that wasn't what interested me most. The place was for sale, and the people to contact were the Matilda S-T Farmer Agency.

24

I drove past the hotel and parked a hundred metres along the street. The Soldiers Arms occupied a corner and I circled around behind it and approached down the side street, keeping to the footpath furthest away. Tall trees blocked some of the view and the sun was in my eyes so I couldn't get much of an idea whether there was anyone inside the place or not. Both streets were narrow and quiet with the usual gentrified terraces and semis that characterise Balmain. There might even be a glimpse of the water from the top level of the tallest houses. Money in the bank. There appeared to be a sizeable yard at the back of the pub, enclosed by a high fence with three strands of barbed wire on top.

I kept moving, trying to register everything without drawing attention to myself. A narrow lane ran behind the yard and there was a driveway beside the building leading out onto the front street. Three possible exits. Hard to imagine a better place to hide, especially if the beer was still on.

This needed thinking about. If I was right about the pub being the hideout, there was no way I was going to charge in there up against Lonsdale and his mate and possibly Wendy and others. I was in the information business, not the crime-busting one. I wanted to know what was planned for the Wombarra properties and who was behind it. That's all Elizabeth Farmer could expect me to do. Anything else would be a bonus.

First thing would be to find out if they were there. Then to isolate someone and get him or her to talk. If Lonsdale had killed MacPherson then he was potentially in bigger trouble than his associates. Might be some leverage there. A patient and cautious person would see it as a watch and wait situation, something I'm not good at. I had to stir the possum somehow. I went back to the car and called Marisha on my mobile.

'So soon,' she said.

'Can you do something for me?'

'Of course.'

I asked her to phone Matilda's agency and express an interest in buying the Soldiers Arms. She should be insistent to the point of rudeness. I told her she could expect to be put off. When that happened, she should say that she and her husband would drive by anyway and take a good look.

'Acting,' she said. 'Fun.'

'Yeah, but do it from a public phone, not from your place or a mobile. When you've done it, call me and let me know how it went.'

She called back in a few minutes. 'I was put on to the boss, a Ms —'

'Hyphen, hyphen. What did she say?'

'She was very discouraging, and the more insistent I became the more discouraging she got. In the end I did as you said.'

'That's great, Marisha. Thanks.'

'That's all?'

'That's a whole lot. I'll tell you about it later.'

I positioned myself with a pair of quality field glasses at a high point back from the hotel. Under a tree, not too conspicuous, could almost have been birdwatching. After a few minutes the big gate to the yard slid open and a figure emerged. He wore a cap and shades and I couldn't identify him. Not Lonsdale, I'd have expected him still to be limping. Maybe his mate, maybe not. He grabbed the handles of the wheelie bin standing a few metres from the gate and pulled it back inside. The gate stood open while he positioned the bin. Long enough for me to see a car parked in the yard. I made a quick adjustment of the focus and got a fix on the numberplate. BMWs look much the same as a lot of other makes, especially at a distance, but this car was fire engine red and bore the registration number De Witt had given me for Wendy's new toy. The gate slid closed smoothly.

First point established. I put the glasses away and leaned back against the tree to ease my still slightly aching bones. I ran the personnel through my mind—Wendy, Lonsdale, the guy with the wheelie bin, Matilda, Buckingham—where was the weakest link? Only one answer to that. I drove to my place, stowed my bag, checked on the mail and sat down with a pot of coffee to think. I ran various scenarios through my head, speculating on their likely outcomes and rejected one after another. It was well on in the afternoon before I'd sorted it out to my satisfaction. I picked out a piece of equipment and headed for Newtown.

I parked as close as I could get to the agency and went up the steps and through the door. The front office was as busy as it had been the time I called wearing my best suit and almost polite manner. Different now.

'Matilda in?' I snapped at one of the women who lifted her head to look at me.

'Yes, but —'

I stepped around the desk and made for the stairs.

'You can't —'

'I can and she'll tell you so in a couple of minutes.'

I went up the stairs and into Matilda S-T Farmer's office without knocking. She looked up as I slammed the door behind me. In drill trousers, boots, army shirt and with my face chopped up she didn't recognise me.

'What do you think you're —'

I strode to her desk and slapped it hard with my hand centimetres away from hers. 'Wendy Jones, Matthew Lonsdale, the Soldiers Arms, the murder of your husband, Larry Buckingham—we've got things to talk about, Matilda. Ring down and tell them no interruptions. Otherwise, it's the police right here and now and they'll be keen to hear what I have to tell them.'

Her perfect makeup and studied composure seemed to crumble at the same time. 'I don't —'

I slammed the desk again. 'Do it! Do it now or someone down there'll get the cops and believe me, you'll be deep in the shit.'

She sucked in air and touched a button on her desk with a perfectly manicured but trembling finger. 'Yes, yes,' she said. 'It's all right, Phoebe. It's all right, really. No calls please, and no interruptions.'

No coffee on a silver tray this time, but issuing orders restored some measure of her authority, in her own eyes at least. She sat straight in her chair and looked at me. She wore a dark, high-necked blouse with a silver brooch at the throat. She passed a hand over her hair although it was immaculate. 'Who the hell are you?'

'You don't recognise me?'

'Should I?'

'Didn't you wonder why Mr Gerard Lees, the security consultant, didn't get back to you about renting office property?'

Her big blue eyes narrowed. 'Jesus Christ. I thought there was something fishy.'

'Doesn't matter now. Shut up and listen.'

I told her who I was and who I was working for, why I'd come to see her initially, and most of what happened subsequently. She blinked a bit at the murder bits but otherwise took it without flinching. I told her that I knew a man wanted by the police for a shotgun killing was holed up in a property owned by Larry Buckingham that was in some sense under her care.

'No, I —'

'Don't bother. A phone call from an associate of mine to you here set things humming at the place. I was watching.'

She shook her head. 'A stupid mistake.'

'I think you've made a few.'

'Possibly. So you're a private detective. You work for money. Perhaps we could come to an arrangement.'

'No, I work for people. Don't even think about it. But there could be a way out of this for you. I'm not sure. It'll depend on what you tell me now.'

She nodded.

'Your firm is connected in some way to Kembla Holdings. Kembla Holdings' principal is Larry Buckingham. His ex-lover is Wendy Jones who's running around with a guy who tried to kill me and did kill someone connected to your husband's Wombarra land.'

'I know nothing about a threat to you or a killing.'

'Maybe. I hope so for your sake. I think you've been instrumental in Buckingham getting hold of the land adjoining your husband's property. It goes without saying that Frederick Farmer's death wasn't an accident.'

I didn't put it very well and she could feel the amount of speculation involved. It gave her confidence. 'I don't know what you're talking about.'

'You do. I've got someone following the money trail. Someone good. The connection's there and she'll find it.'

'Bugger you!'

'What would Phoebe think if she heard language like that? Here's the real question, Tilly—why does Buckingham want the land so badly that he has one, maybe two people killed for it?'

She was more composed again now, although she suddenly looked a lot older, more like her real age than the one she could easily pass for when she had everything fully under control. Her hands were clasped together in front of her on the desk with her elbows tucked in as if she needed physical as well as mental control. The precise, up-market voice that had slipped momentarily when she'd sworn was back in place. She sat very still. She wasn't one of those people who needed to make a show of thinking, weighing things up. No wrinkling of the brow, no scratching of the chin. She just did it.

'Before I answer that,' she said, 'let me tell you something. God, I don't even know your name.'

'Hardy.'

'Mr Hardy. I have had what could politely be called a "past". To be blunt, I was a stripper when I was young and a call girl when I was a bit older. I did . . . performances for police functions and for footballers. I have two convictions for prostitution and one for wounding. That was when a client got out of hand. I served a short sentence. Larry Buckingham was present at a couple of my strip shows and he has photographs. He also has friends in the police and found out about my convictions. When he saw notices of my marriage to Frederick and read that I had established this business, he got in touch with me. As well as the photographs he has statements from some of my former clients and the police records. Frederick Farmer was a very straitlaced man and you cannot hold a real estate agent's licence if you have a criminal record. Buckingham's been blackmailing me virtually since the day of my marriage.'

'He got you to provide a hideout for Wendy and company?'

'Yes.'

'And forged some link between your company and one of his?'

'Yes.'

'That's all very interesting,' I said. 'But you haven't answered my question. Why does Buckingham want the land?'

She clasped and unclasped her hands. She wore rings on several fingers of both hands and they grated together. 'I swear to you that I don't know.'

I didn't want to, but I believed her. It had cost her a lot to say what she'd said to a total stranger and a hostile one at that, and it wasn't something she'd do lightly. She could see herself getting into another tight spot when she was already in one. I reckoned that a good part of what she'd said was the truth.

'What's Buckingham like?'

'He's a brute.'

'Couldn't you . . . manipulate him?'

She smiled but there was no humour in it. 'When I was younger, maybe. I'm talking about much younger, like, say, thirteen. But I was still a good girl at thirteen.'

'He and Wendy Jones were lovers, I'm told.'

'Yes, she's how old, would you say?'

I thought about the showy entrance she'd made at the casino in her red dress and all the trimmings. Probably looked older than she was. 'Mid-twenties, maybe.'

'A bit less, and her time with Larry was at least ten years ago.'

'They're still connected?'

'Yes, in some way. I wouldn't be surprised if she's got something on him the way he has on me. She's got some pretty tough friends, unlike me.'

'Again, that's interesting,' I said. 'Tell me more about Wendy. How do you know her?'

'I've been Larry's . . . companion a couple of times when he's needed someone he could rely on to keep her mouth shut and who wasn't about one-third of his age. He introduced me to Wendy.'

'What sort of occasions?'

'It'd be more than my life's worth to tell you.'

'Meeting someone isn't knowing them. You seem to know a lot about her.'

'Not really, but she approached me after Frederick died with an offer to buy the place. They assumed that I'd inherited it rather than Elizabeth. I was curious and strung her along. We met a couple of times. Then I told her the truth.'

'How'd she take it?'

'Badly. She looks . . . well, you know how she looks with those ghastly jewel implants, but she's a shrewd young woman.'

'Do you think she'd know what's behind all this?'

She shrugged. The talking had restored her confidence more than I would have wanted. 'Possibly,' she said. 'Probably.'

'You're going to have to help me find a way to isolate her and put her under pressure.'

'No. I'd be much too afraid.'

I reached into my shirt pocket and took out a miniature tape recorder. I pressed the buttons and played back my last words and hers. 'Your future,' I said.

25

She was a woman who'd played a role for some time and had probably coped with some difficult moments in that role. This was harder. She kept her cool, but I imagined I could see the conflicting possibilities working behind her smooth façade. She could bluff, try tears or maybe her feminine appeal, of which there was plenty. Nothing in my manner would have encouraged those options. You can't make the jump from stripper to real estate queen without being pragmatic and resourceful. My guess was that Matilda Sharpe-Tarleton Farmer would do her best to turn the situation to her own advantage.

'What do you have in mind?'

'I need to talk to Wendy, one on one. Put certain propositions to her.'

She shook her head. 'I doubt you can do that. I don't know anything much about what went on and I don't want to know, but I do know that Wendy wants to lie low for quite a while. She's frightened, I think, but she's the kind of woman who's dangerous when she's frightened.'

'It's worth a try,' I said. 'Ring her and tell her that the coast is clear at the hotel—the would-be buyers aren't keen.

Then you say Elizabeth Farmer is interested in selling her land but will only talk to her.'

'Elizabeth doesn't know Wendy.'

'But Wendy knows about her and how important the land is. She knows Elizabeth has been using me to sniff around. I could've told her about Wendy and now she's playing it her way. She'll bite. She'll contact Buckingham and he'll tell her to do it. He wants the place that badly.'

'It might work but I'd be taking a big risk if it doesn't. Buckingham would ruin me. What guarantee do I have that he won't anyway, however it turns out?'

'Not much of one, but look at it this way. If you don't do it I'll give this tape to the police who'll want to question you about some of the admissions you've made on it— harbouring criminals, for example. And your agent's licence is history. Part of the bent cop connection Buckingham's got in the Illawarra has come apart and it's likely some of those cops'll start singing.'

'That's not much reassurance.'

I shrugged. 'With a lot of luck this could finish him. He's already in trouble and he desperately wants that land for some big deal or other. That's why he'll tell Wendy to do what he says. The signs are that the land thing is his big play. If it doesn't come off, chances are he's stuffed and he'll be too busy to worry about you. Or not able to do you much harm anyway.'

'He'll harm me. Bet on it.'

'I'll put in a good word for you.'

She snorted, sounding more like the old Tilly than the new model. 'It all sounds very iffy to me, but you've probably got enough nerve to pull it off. All right. I haven't got much choice. I'll do it.'

. . .

I gave her explicit instructions and she made the call. She played it straight and Wendy asked for some time as I expected she would. Matilda hung up looking strained around the eyes. This was tougher than flogging decaying terraces to yuppies.

'You did that well,' I said. 'But you shot me a look just before you said "Never heard of him". Was that what I think it was?'

'Yes. She was asking if I'd had any contact with you.'

'Okay. She'll be ringing Buckingham now.'

'I bet you wish you could hear the conversation.'

'You're right. But I'll tell her the hotel phones are bugged and I have heard it.'

'You're a devious bastard. That'll put me in still deeper. My calls here must be piling up. Do you think I could do a little work?'

'You've got some nerve yourself.'

She shrugged. 'Life must go on. I've got a feeling I'm going to need every cent I can find when this washes up. Whoever wins.'

Pragmatic to the max. She had it right—it felt like a contest between Buckingham and me. 'After Wendy calls back,' I said.

She fidgeted and I tried not to while we waited for half an hour. The call came and Wendy agreed to come to the agency at six o'clock to meet with Elizabeth Farmer. I told Matilda to make her calls and to be sure they were about the real estate business and nothing else. I'd be listening. I also told her to get one of her minions to bring up some coffee and to make sure none of them worked overtime.

The coffee arrived and although the woman bringing it looked surprised at the company her boss was keeping, she didn't comment. Matilda busied herself and I tried to get Elizabeth Farmer on my mobile to put her in the picture but she wasn't answering at the university or at home. Maybe getting in a quick nine holes before dark. My next call was to Hank Bachelor, the young American working part-time for a security outfit and doing the TAFE private eye course. I keep him on a small retainer for backup work. If Wendy arrived with one of her mates I wanted to know about it. I gave Hank the time and the address and the descriptions.

'You want information, Cliff, or action?'

'If she's got a mate with a bazooka you'd better shoot him, otherwise just let me know.'

'Got it.'

Matilda looked at me across her desk. 'You've thought this all out, haven't you?'

'Tried to, but shit happens.'

'You never said a truer word. Elizabeth hates me, doesn't she?'

'I think that's fair to say.'

'Dykes,' she muttered and got back to her work.

Time went by; a couple of the office staff came in for quick consultations; Matilda's phone rang and she answered it; she made some calls; the working day ended. At five forty-five I heard a buzzing and clicking.

'Last one to leave sets the security alarm,' Matilda said.

'Okay, let's go down and disarm it. You can buzz people in, right?'

'Yes.'

We dealt with the alarm and went back to her office. 'When she rings, you let her in. Then you call her up here.'

'Then what?'

'Then we see how it goes.'

At a minute to six my mobile rang.

'Cliff, blonde chick on a Harley. No passenger.'

The intercom cut in as the call ended. 'Matilda? It's Wendy.'

Matilda pressed a button. I was standing at the open door near the top of the stairs and heard the door lock release. Boots scraped on the polished wood floor. I waved at Matilda.

'Up here, Wendy,' Matilda called.

She came up the stairs with a springy step and took a long stride into the room. I was behind the door. I tripped her and she fell hard. I had a pair of plastic restraints ready and I had them on her with her arms behind her back before she could draw breath. When she did, she snarled and spat.

'What the fuck . . . ?'

'Shut up,' I said. I grabbed her by the collar of her leather jacket and heaved her into a chair. Her eyes blazed at me and the jewel implants in her teeth glittered.

'You're Hardy,' she said.

'That's right. Nice to meet you.'

'Matilda, you're fuckin' dead.'

I told her to shut up again and laid it out pretty much as I had for Matilda but with a different spin. I emphasised her association with Lonsdale and the evidence the police had on him in connection with the MacPherson killing. I told her about Barton and Henderson and the attempt on my life and how I thought Larry Buckingham was involved with them and with the killing of Tom Purcell, the under-cover cop.

'I'm sure you know him by some other name, Wendy. Tough little guy, drove a beat-up Land Cruiser. Hung around dealing dope at that shitty racetrack you bikies use.'

'Dunno what you're talking about.'

'Then there's the bugs in the telephones at the hotel. Should be some interesting stuff there. You and Buckingham.'

She didn't react, just listened, occasionally running her tongue over her teeth jewels. I had to play the ace.

'I've got a witness who saw you acting suspiciously around a house under the scarp in Wombarra. House burned down and a man died in the fire. She can identify you. That's a big one, Wendy.'

That got her attention. 'What the fuck d'you want?'

I leaned closer to her. She smelled of sweat and cigarettes and some of the sweat was fresh. 'That stuff about the fire doesn't have to come out,' I said. 'I can control that. And Lonsdale was acting under Buckingham's instructions, not yours. You can probably get clear of all this. All I want from you is information.'

She licked the jewels again, then her lips. She looked across at Matilda, who turned her head away. 'Like what?'

'Why does Larry Buckingham want those pieces of land?'

The way she chewed the question over told me that she knew the answer. I felt a surge of excitement at being so close to it.

'You'll let me go if I tell you?'

'Yeah. Might take a while and Lonsdale has to go down, but with a bit of luck you can drive off in your Beemer, win some more dough at the casino.'

She smiled. 'Mattie Lonsdale'd like to meet you again

after what you did to him in the car park. His knee's buggered.'

'Too bad. Well, what's it to be?'

Before she could answer my mobile rang again. I swore, took it out and answered it. 'Hank?'

'No Hank here, Hardy. This is Larry Buckingham.'

I didn't say anything.

'Still there, Hardy?'

'Yes.'

'I believe you've got my girl Wendy and my girl Matilda there with you, that right?'

'Yes again.'

'That's cool, because I'm sitting here with your girl Dr Elizabeth Farmer and she's not looking too happy. I'd say we have to talk, wouldn't you?'

26

I never was much of a poker player and the women could see that something had gone wrong. My knuckles whitened as I gripped the phone. 'Say what you have to say.'

Wendy grinned. 'It's Larry, isn't it?'

'Shut up!'

'Hey,' Buckingham said. 'I can hear Wendy. Tell her everything's going to be all right.'

'Larry!' Wendy Jones yelled.

'Sounds like you got a control problem there, Hardy. Everything's under control here at the doc's place. I just have to ask the doc a few questions. I'll get back to you.'

'Wait.'

He hung up. Wendy was jigging in her chair. 'He's too smart for you, dickhead. Get these fuckin' things off me.'

'What is it, Hardy?' Matilda said quietly.

'He's got Elizabeth. How I don't know, but it gives him the upper hand.'

'You bet it does,' Wendy said. 'He's not the gentlest guy with women. I oughta know. You better do as he says.'

'He hasn't said anything yet.'

Matilda came close to biting her manicured nails. 'You'd

better let us both go. I'll have to put distance between me and him, and you should go and help Elizabeth.'

'Fuck her and you too,' Wendy said.

I said nothing, thinking hard to no purpose. The phone rang again.

'Yes?'

'Cliff, Cliff can you come, please?'

'Elizabeth. Has he hurt you?'

'No, I've hurt him. Tania came waltzing in and distracted him. I hit him with a five iron. He's unconscious. He had a gun. I was so frightened.'

I could feel the smile spreading across my face. 'How badly is he hurt?'

'Tania says he's concussed. She's done first aid. What should we do? I think there's a man outside. Tania says she saw someone.'

'Lock the doors and call the police and an ambulance. I'll be there before them and I'll help you handle it. It'll be all right.'

'Hurry.'

'I will.' I hung up. Wendy wasn't looking so chipper now. 'Sorry, ladies, the tables have turned again. Elizabeth clobbered him with a golf club and he's out cold. The cops are on their way.'

Matilda recovered first. 'What now, Hardy?'

'You both stay here. The deal's still on.' I rang Hank's mobile and told him he was needed. He buzzed and I let him in. Hank stands at about 190 centimetres and is wide. He filled the doorway.

'I want you to entertain these ladies while I'm away. Could be a while.'

'Lucky I brought my mouth harp,' Hank said.

I went down the stairs and out at a dead run. Elizabeth's house was only minutes away by car and I pulled up outside to see a guy standing uncertainly by the gate. I hopped out and let him see the .38 in my hand.

'Your boss's inside with his head stove in. The cops are on their way. Do you want to stick around and talk to them or would you rather piss off?'

He looked at me, then at the gun, walked to a white Merc standing nearby and drove off without a word. I went through the gate and knocked on the door.

'Elizabeth, it's Hardy.'

The door opened slowly and Tania beckoned me in. We went down the passage to the sitting room. One wall was blood spattered. A big, dark-haired man was lying face up on the floor. The light-coloured rug was stained around his head. He wore a suit and tie and the tie had been loosened at his fat neck. Larry Buckingham had put on a lot of weight since his playing days. His eyes were closed but his chest was moving.

Elizabeth Farmer sat in a chair beside him, her hands still gripping the club. The adrenalin that had energised her when she made the phone call had gone. Her normally high, healthy colour had drained away leaving her sheet white. She looked worse than Buckingham. A pistol lay on the floor, half under a chair.

'You called the police and the ambulance?'

Tania nodded. 'Elizabeth, Cliff's here. It's all right.'

Elizabeth stared at me sightlessly. 'I'm a teacher,' she said slowly. 'A scholar. I hate violence. I don't hit people.'

'This man played a part in the death of your father,' I said. 'I wouldn't blame you if you hit him again.'

She shuddered. 'This is awful. Awful.'

'It'd be a lot worse if you hadn't hit him. Tania, can you get her some brandy or something? And something for me as well.'

Tania stepped around Buckingham and bent down to kiss Elizabeth's cheek. 'You were wonderful, darling. I'm proud of you.'

Before the troops arrived, I phoned Farrow in Wollongong and began to tell him what had happened. He cut me off.

'You've got him?'

'He's lying here with a very sore head. Just beginning to come around.'

'Hang on to him. Barton's been talking. Larry Buckingham's in big trouble.'

'The uniforms'll be here soon,' I said. 'Dr Farmer and I'll have some explaining to do.'

'Call me the minute they arrive and let me talk to the senior guy. I'll set him straight. What happened?'

I gave Farrow a quick summary and he was still on the line when the police and the ambulance arrived. The cops took a look at the scene and knew they needed help. I handed the mobile to the one who looked least shocked.

'I've got Inspector Farrow from Wollongong CID on the line. He wants to talk to you.'

The cop looked relieved. He took the phone, identified himself and listened. He said yes several times and looked at Buckingham and the paramedics.

'He seems to be okay, sir. Yes, the woman's distressed but unharmed. There's a pistol on the floor. No, we won't. Yes, sir, he'll go to hospital under guard.'

He handed back the phone and wiped sweat from his

face with the back of his hand. Inner-city cops see all kinds of things but this must have been unusual—an up-market terrace, a villain on the floor, blood and a gun, two women clinging to each other and a battered male with a .38 stuck in his belt and a tumbler of brandy in his hand.

'Shit,' he said. 'What a mess.'

'Constable,' I said. 'It looks just fine to me.'

Elizabeth and Tania were close together on the arm of a chair, both with brandy in glasses, as the paramedics worked on Buckingham. They examined the wound on his head, stabilised his neck in a brace and got ready to slide him onto a stretcher.

'How is he?' I said.

One of them looked up. 'Severely concussed; no fracture. Needs stitches. Pretty tough bloke. Think I recognise him—Larry Buckingham, played for the Tigers.'

'In the good old days,' I said. 'Hello, his eyes are open. Better strap him down.'

They eased the stretcher under Buckingham and ran heavy straps over and under. Locked them. Buckingham stared up at me, trying to focus.

'G'day, Larry,' I said. 'Didn't quite work out your way.'

His pale lips moved but I couldn't catch what he said. I stared down at him—a hundred plus kilos of fat and muscle and money devoted to creating havoc in the world. Reduced to this. I thought of the lives he'd cost and the ones he'd damaged and I was almost sorry that Elizabeth Farmer hadn't hit him harder and somewhere fatal.

'I'm told you like your women young, Larry,' I said. 'Pity you came up against a real one.'

27

Detectives from Newtown arrived and it took another couple of calls to Farrow to sort things out with them. Eventually Buckingham was carted off and the cops departed. I was left alone with the two women and the depleted brandy bottle. Elizabeth was coming out of her mildly shocked state but looked ready to keel over pretty soon. Clear-headed Tania wanted to know everything down to the last detail.

'I haven't got to it yet,' I said. 'But I'm going back now to talk to the person who's got the answers, with no reason not to tell me. In fact she's got every reason to tell me.'

'Who's that?' Tania said.

'Wendy Jones.' I tapped my front teeth with the tumbler. 'You remember her, at the casino.'

'Oh, yeah—the hard-faced blonde.'

'That's her.' I drained the last of the brandy and stood up. 'Are you going to be okay, Elizabeth?'

Tania put her hand on Elizabeth's shoulder. 'Of course she's okay. She's the heroine of this episode, isn't she? You were a bit slack, letting him get to her like that.'

'Tania,' Elizabeth said.

'No, you're right. I tried to contact Elizabeth to get her to lay low while this plan of mine went down but I couldn't reach her. I should've tried harder.'

'I was on the course.'

'Practice makes perfect,' I said. 'Great five iron.'

Elizabeth's face lit up—she was Germaine Greer the younger again.

I'd had two solid belts of brandy on an empty stomach and was feeling the effects as I drove the short distance back to Matilda's office. I scanned the street carefully after I parked but there was no activity out of the normal. I'd told the cops where Lonsdale and his mate were hiding and they should've been in the bag by now. No reason to think Buckingham still had cards to play, but best to be sure. I hit the bell and announced myself. The door clicked and I went up to Matilda's office. My feet wanted to drag a bit on the stairs and I realised that I was tired, physically and mentally, at a deep level. But I fought the feeling off, helped by the brandy buzz. I sucked in some deep breaths and went into the office.

Nothing had changed. Matilda was still behind her desk and Wendy was in the armchair. Hank sat in a chair tilted back against the wall.

'Dull party,' he said. 'You bring some take-out, Cliff?'

'No. You can go, mate. Many thanks.'

He let his chair drop and slipped out of it in his athletic fashion. 'Ladies,' he said and went out.

Wendy shifted in obvious discomfort. 'My hands are numb, you fuck.'

I perched on the edge of the desk. 'Won't be long. Larry's gone off to hospital with a concussion—'

'Bullshit,' Wendy said, but she didn't mean it.

'It's true. Dr Elizabeth Farmer, Associate Professor of Linguistics, got him with a five iron about here.' I touched the spot above my right ear. 'Dropped him like a stone. Severe concussion, according to the paramedic. I had a word with the Wollongong cops as they were wheeling him out. Like I told you, Barton's been talking and put Larry right in it. He'll be under guard and there'll be some charges. I'd guess supplying drugs, accessory to murder, maybe more. He's gone.'

'He'll still have some reach from prison.'

'That'll be your problem. As far as I'm concerned if you tell me what I want to know and make it convincing, you walk away from the arson charge and the association with Lonsdale and Buckingham and Barton and the whole bunch.'

Wendy looked at Matilda, who offered her nothing. Wendy was tired and the events of the night had taken a big toll on her. She licked the jewelled teeth but it was just a habit now, not a statement. 'Okay. Larry wanted the land on account of the mine shafts. There's going to be much less traffic up around there now that the coast road's closed for a couple of years. The mines run right back under the scarp and come up near the surface on the other side where he owns some more land. He reckoned to tunnel down to meet up with the shafts. No big deal. His idea was to set up a speed and ecstasy lab and a hydroponic dope operation underground. He's already got all the gear—generators, pumps and all that. It's in a police garage in Thirroul some-where. He could build up a bloody great plant well out of sight and ship the stuff out from his own private property. It'd be worth millions.'

I watched her and mulled it over. Her behaviour was believable enough. What about the information? It sounded convincing. Our natural tendency is to think about what's above the ground, what we can see, rather than what's below and hidden from us. Two ways in and out from something totally concealed. I could buy it.

'If he finds out I told you he'll kill me.'

'Oh, I don't know. Could've been Matilda.'

Matilda shot from her chair. 'No, I didn't know anything about it.'

'So you say.' I took out my Swiss army knife and cut the plastic restraints. 'I wouldn't worry too much, Wendy. Larry's got to have a lot else on his mind.'

She brought her hands around to the front slowly and massaged her wrists. 'Yeah. He's got investors. They're not going to be happy.'

'I hope they squeeze him hard. You're going to need some leverage, Wendy. Matilda suggested you had something on Buckingham. I hope that's true.'

'You bet it is. Thinking about it, I'm more worried about the cops than Larry. Can I go?'

I closed the knife. 'Yep. Just to keep you focused, I dunno about the Beemer though. I told the cops where Lonsdale and his mate were hiding. They've probably picked them up by now but you'd be taking a risk to go back there for the car. I suppose there's some of your stuff there as well. Might have to settle for a quick flit on the Harley. Up to you.'

'You bastard.'

I shrugged. 'Hock your teeth.'

She gave me a look that would've stripped paint. She squared her shoulders, zipped her jacket and marched from the room. I nodded to Matilda and she released the door to the street. Minutes later I could hear the angry roar of the Harley engine as it fired up.

Matilda reached down to her bag, took out a compact and lipstick, repaired her makeup. Her hands moved over her hair as she groomed herself like a cat. When she was satisfied she got up and came around the desk. She sat down next to me, letting me latch on to her perfume and the warmth of her body.

'So you've won.'

'Looks that way. Pretty good for a dyke, eh—what Elizabeth did?'

She nodded. 'But you don't seem very happy about it all.'

'A couple of good people are dead. That silly bikie bitch'll cause more trouble before she's through. Buckingham's presumably got plenty of money. He'll buy a QC who'll work the system. He'll sell out his investors. Let's say they're Asians. Call them terrorists. That'll play with the powers that be. He'll do some time, but it'll be easy time.'

Her soft hand was touching one of the scabs on my cheek. 'So why d'you bother?'

I removed the hand. 'You should've seen the look on your stepdaughter's face when it all got sorted.'

She stiffened and drew away. 'And as for me?'

'As for you, Tilly,' I said, 'you'd better hope Buckingham doesn't decide to lower the boom on you. But I wouldn't count on it.'

Her shoulders drooped and she seemed to shrink inside

her smart suit and classy blouse. 'I've got no one to turn to,' she said.

I eased myself stiffly up off the desk and stretched. Despite all the knocks and hurts I felt invigorated. I bent, collected the cut restraints and put them in my pocket. 'That's the penalty for loving yourself more than anyone else,' I said.

28

What I'd said to Matilda was sound enough, I thought as I drove towards Glebe. Trouble was, I couldn't help thinking it might apply to me. It was too late and too much had happened too quickly to make such thoughts useful. On auto pilot, I got back home, parked and had the key in the door before I remembered Marisha. Had I promised to go back there? I couldn't remember.

Sometimes, after a case has come together, I feel like a creature that should be in hibernation being forced to carry on beyond its allotted time. Not tonight. My brain wouldn't stop working. I felt bad about exposing Elizabeth Farmer to that danger, relieved, but at the same time embarrassed by how well she'd coped. I sat down and wrote her a long report on all the aspects of the case. My suspicion that her father had been killed because he'd got an inkling of Buckingham's plan had no foundation in fact and probably never would have, but it felt right. I said that I'd had to offer Matilda a certain amount of protection in return for her cooperation in isolating Wendy. That wouldn't please her. It would please her even less that I'd let Wendy off the hook, since I was sure she'd been involved in the arson.

Again, necessity, but it didn't sit well with me and I made
no reference to it.

I read the report through when I'd finished and was dis-
satisfied. It was plausible, in the true meaning of the word.
I emailed De Witt, telling him about Buckingham's plan as
I'd promised to do. It'd be up to him to decide how to use
it. If he went into print on it the police wouldn't be pleased
and would probably heavy him. I'd have to hope he adhered
to the journalists' code of ethics and protected his source.

As I finished the email and before I sent it, the phone
rang. Farrow.

'How's it looking?' I said.

'Okay. We picked up Lonsdale and another guy at the
hotel. No sign of Wendy Jones. Where is she, Hardy?'

'Don't you want to know what Larry Buckingham's
grand plan was?'

'Sure.'

I told him. From his silence I guessed that it was news
to him, but still I asked, 'Did you get a sniff of that from
Barton?'

'I can't discuss operational police matters with you.'

'Means you didn't. Well, be my guest. You'll find a lot
of equipment for that project. A little bird tells me it's in
Thirroul.'

'Let's back up. Where's Wendy?'

'No idea. That's the truth.'

'You keep that information about the mine shafts to
yourself, Hardy.'

He hung up and I sat looking at my message to De Witt
on the screen. I certainly owed Farrow; but for him I was
buried under a ton of earth and a layer of aggregate down
Port Kembla way. But I remembered what he'd said about

the way things could play out with the prosecution of Barton and the other corrupt cops, and I'd already had my thoughts about what Larry Buckingham could contrive if he had the money.

I hit send, and dispatched the email.

De Witt's story made the Wollongong and Sydney papers in the morning. He had some of the names and some of the details—enough to give the story flavour and show how a major episode in criminal organisation and police corruption had been orchestrated and exposed. I wasn't mentioned except as a 'source' and that was fine by me. Buckingham was in hospital but under arrest with a battery of charges pending. There were photographs of him in his athletic heyday and in his bloated present. Barton wasn't mentioned by name, suggesting that a deal was being done. Par for the course.

Marisha rang me mid-morning.

'That was your case, wasn't it, Cliff?'

'What case would that be?'

'Please don't think I'm stupid. I read the paper. I know my car was down there in Wollongong. The police told me.'

'You're right. Sorry, Marisha, I don't like to talk about the work. You never know about loose ends, people wanting to get even in some way. It's best to keep your friends right out of it.'

'Is that what we are, friends?'

'I don't know, Marisha. I'm sorry. It takes a while to come down from these things. I've been dealing with shot-guns and dead men and wild women and crooked cops and it—'

'Sorry, sorry, sorry, and wog drama queens and teenage whores. I understand.'

'Marisha—'

She hung up. I had her number and I could've called back. Maybe she wanted me to, maybe she didn't. I wavered, but I didn't call. I sat, looking at the phone and remembering. What I'd said was true. I'd got into relationships with women in the middle of cases before and, mostly, they hadn't gone anywhere. There's something about the situation, the pressures, the need for comfort and release that can shape your feelings and distort your judgement. One of the penalties of the business, something Cyn had sensed early in our marriage, was that dealing in deceit and mistrust, violence and hurt, so much of the time erodes the ability to believe in anything human. Chinks open in the armour; there are moments and times of love and trust, but they don't last because the job busts in and cuts them down.

I tried my usual therapy—a long walk around Glebe, clocking the improvements and the damage and diverting my-self by trying to decide where the balance lay. On those occasions when I judged that the ledger worked out in the black, I felt encouraged, other times, not. Today, I was somewhere in the middle and that wasn't unusual. I tramped back along Glebe Point Road thinking that this was pretty much the way I regarded the state of the country as a whole—good impulses on the part of the many, rotten motives from the few who held the power, for now. The whole thing in the balance. No help there.

I turned into my street and felt an uplift when I saw Aaron De Witt's stately old Volvo station wagon, dust-streaked and dented, parked outside my house. It was late enough for a drink for me and to brew up a strong coffee for De Witt. There were things he could tell me and things I could tell him. I was grateful for his concealment of my identity behind the mask of the 'source'. Made me feel like Deep Throat, whoever he or she was.

I approached the car on the driver's side. It was empty. Probably taking a stroll around while he waited for me, I thought. I went inside, leaving the gate and the front door open, and put the coffee on. I opened a bottle of white and sampled it. Good enough to drink. I took the glass out to the front and leaned on the gate looking up and down the street. I finished the drink and went back inside for a refresher. Still no sign of De Witt after about twenty minutes.

I put the glass down and went out to take a closer look at the car. Back and front seats empty. The windows to the utility area at the back were too dirty to see through so I opened the back doors. Long, lanky Aaron De Witt was compressed and folded in a foetal position along with some tools and a couple of children's toys. I recognised him from his clothing and from the nicotine-stained hand that lay lifelessly clear of the body. His features had been mostly obliterated by a shotgun blast.

So again it was a long session with police and more contact with Farrow and eventually the arrival of a TV crew and me losing my temper with the reporter and only just holding back from assaulting him in the presence of police. The SOC officers did their thing; the ambulance took the body away and a tow truck carted off De Witt's vehicle.

I was left standing by my gate with Aronson from the Glebe station, who'd done the liaising with Farrow. He wasn't sympathetic.

'I said you were a nuisance, Hardy, and I meant it. You got that guy killed.'

I'd only just missed being killed myself, and so, probably, had my client, but it didn't seem like the time to point that out. I didn't say anything.

Aronson looked at my house with its cracked cement path, lifting porch tiles, warped wrought iron fence and sagging guttering. He shook his head. 'How many people are sorry they ever met you?'

'Too many,' I said.

I went back inside the house with a strange sense of loss for someone I scarcely knew. I felt responsible as well, even though I knew De Witt was a volunteer. The coffee I'd prepared for him reproached me. I poured a mug and added a slug of whisky. No matter what they say, you can use alcohol to take the edge off mental as well as physical pain. I sat in the sun in the back courtyard and let its warmth and the warmth of the whisky run through me. I was close to feeling better when I thought of Elizabeth. I rushed inside and called her, first at home, then at the university, getting answering machines at both numbers. I left the same message—go somewhere else and be very careful. Ring me when you can.

I went upstairs and turned the computer on, thinking she might have emailed me in response to my report. There was no message from her but there was one from De Witt.

Hi Cliff
Guess you've read the papers. Big scoop and you'll see I
kept you out of it. I'm coming up to Sydney today on
another story but I'll hunt you up. Things to tell you,
like about how MacPherson set up the right sort of
insurance policy for Frederick Farmer and Buckingham
got nervous when he heard you were looking for him
and took steps. Stuff like that. See you soon.
ADeW

I stared at the message and a sick feeling came over me that
no amount of sunshine or whisky would cure.

Elizabeth phoned later in the day. She'd read my report and
got my message. She said she'd moved into a room in the
Women's College and wanted to know why. I told her about
De Witt.

'That's terrible. Poor man.'

'Yes. I don't know that you're in danger but best to make
sure. I'll find out how things stand with Buckingham and
the police and let you know.'

She said she didn't mind living in the college for a
while; it'd be good for her work and Tania was away in
Melbourne.

'Did Tania do that research we spoke about?'

'I think she did a bit. She emailed me. I'll forward it
to you.'

It occurred to me that Matilda might need a warning as
well and I phoned the office and got Phoebe.

'Ms Farmer has gone to the United States on business.'

'Good idea,' I said. 'Think I might do the same.'

'Sir?'

'Never mind. When she gets back tell her Cliff Hardy sent his best wishes.'

29

My relations with Farrow, damaged after I gave so much of the story to De Witt, mended over time because of his need to get my input on certain things, like where Buckingham's equipment was stored and the location of the abandoned mines he'd been interested in. Farrow was able to put pressure on Lonsdale by saying that I'd give evidence against him on charges of abduction and attempted murder. Lonsdale gave up Buckingham as the issuer of the order to kill MacPherson and named the policeman who'd killed Purcell. Larry Buckingham was neatly parcelled and stamped 'to be kept out of circulation for a very long time'. The murder of Aaron De Witt was never sheeted home to anyone but the police and journalists had their suspicions and press treatment of Buckingham was not kind.

Elizabeth Farmer was able to get her life back to normal and to pay me generously for the work I'd done. There was no prosecution for the murder of her father but she had what she called 'closure'. Ever the academic, Elizabeth. Tania had established some corporate connections between Matilda and Buckingham but there was no point in pressing those buttons.

At first I thought that Sue Holland was going to be a sort of casualty of the affair because, as Buckingham's business interests were targeted, there were no funds to complete the sale. But it didn't turn out like that. The contract enabled her to keep the deposit, a handy amount, and she rang me to tell me about it.

'I didn't really want to leave,' she said. 'And now I've got some cash to splash about on improving the place.'

'Good for you,' I said. 'Did you know your mine shaft goes right under the scarp?'

'Who cares?'

Wendy Jones had disappeared, but not too long later I got an envelope in the mail. It had a Queensland postmark and no return address. There was a crude drawing of a motor-cycle on the back of the packet. And a computer disk inside. With some difficulty I got it to open on my computer. The disc contained about thirty images of Buckingham and another man engaged in sexual activity with underage females. The other man was big and blond. Scandinavian. Mostly, the victim was Wendy herself, but there were half a dozen images of a girl tricked out in school uniform. The kid with the blonde plaits and the garish makeup was Kristina Karatsky. I'd never laid eyes on him, but the suspicion leapt into my mind that the other performer was Stefan Parnevik.

A note, smudged and greasy, was attached: 'It's all on his hard disk'. Wendy was well and truly pulling the plug on Larry.

I closed the file and sat looking at the screen, pretty much as I had after reading Aaron De Witt's email that had come to me like a message from the other side. Should I turn the disk over to the cops and put one more nail in Buckingham's coffin? Was it necessary? Would a police investigation turn up Kristina's identity? What consequences could that have? But most of all I wondered about Marisha Karatsky and Kristina and Stefan Parnevik and Buckingham. And everything that Karen Bach had told me about the Karatsky women. All the old suspicions were back in full strength.

Over the next couple of days I phoned Marisha and listened to her answering machine message until I could recite it in my sleep. After about a week she answered.

'Yes, who is this?'

'It's Cliff Hardy, Marisha.'

'Ah, the leaver of no message. A no-show.'

'That's right. Well, I'm showing now. I've been wondering how you were.'

'Now that your case is over and all the loose ends . . . tied off?'

'Yes. Sort of.'

'You don't sound very sure. Well, I'm fine. I've been to New Zealand, you see. It's a beautiful country with a very good government.'

'So they tell me.'

'You've never been there?'

'No.'

'That's strange. In Europe, you visit the neighbouring countries if you can. Why don't Australians visit New Zealand very much?'

You're playing with me, I thought. 'I don't know.'

'You should.'

'Okay.'

'Well, I met with Kristina and she's fine. She's finished with Stefan who has gone somewhere else, and she is studying and working as a ski instructor in Auckland.'

'Is there snow now in Auckland?'

'Of course not. This is an indoor training facility. In the season she'll work at the ski resorts.'

'That sounds good.'

'Yes. So how are you?'

The distance between us was ten times greater than between Sydney and Auckland. I told her I was okay and doing routine stuff.

'I'm moving there. To New Zealand. Perhaps you could visit.'

'Perhaps.'

The conversation ended there and left me more doubtful than ever. It just sounded too pat. You don't get rid of a character like Parnevik so easily—that's if you *want* to get rid of him. I sent Marisha an invoice but it came back marked 'not known at this address'. She wasn't having her mail forwarded to New Zealand, if that's where she'd gone. I wiped the disk, deciding that I'd never really understood Marisha Karatsky.

MORE GOOD BOOKS FROM ALLEN & UNWIN

MASTER'S MATES

PETER CORRIS

When rich, attractive Lorraine Master hires Cliff Hardy to investigate the circumstances surrounding her husband's conviction for smuggling heroin from New Caledonia, Hardy welcomes the assignment. A week on generous expenses sniffing about under a tropical sky, escape from a cold, dry spell in Sydney – just the job. But Stewart Master's mates in Noumea prove to be a difficult and dangerous bunch.

The danger follows Hardy back to Sydney where he and his client become targets when an intricate conspiracy goes seriously wrong. Hardy deals with a tricky lawyer, a man on the run and Sydney's most corrupt ex-cop. He has allies as well, but in the end his survival will depend on his own guts, experience and savvy.

Peter Corris's world weary but always charismatic hero Cliff Hardy has long been established as Australia's favourite investigator. Often bloodied but never bowed in this latest gripping novel, Hardy's legions of fans will relish another pacy adventure, branching further afield than his traditional mean streets territory to the steamy island paradise of French New Caledonia.

ISBN 1 74114 136 2

MORE GOOD BOOKS FROM ALLEN & UNWIN

THE EMPTY BEACH

Cliff Hardy Classics

PETER CORRIS

The early 1980s found Cliff Hardy well established as a private investigator but still battling his demons. He has quit smoking and moderated his drinking. The memory of his brief marriage still haunts him along with other ghosts from his past.

A case in Bondi attracts him as an ex-surfer and admirer of the suburb. It began as a routine investigation into a supposed drowning. But Hardy soon finds himself literally fighting for his life in the murky, violent underworld of Bondi.

The truth about John Singer, black marketeer and poker machine king is out there somewhere – amidst the drug addicts, prostitutes and alcoholics. Hardy's job is to stay alive long enough in that world of easy death to get to the truth.

The truth hurts . . .

ISBN 1 74114 180 X

MORE GOOD BOOKS FROM ALLEN & UNWIN

THE VERGE PRACTICE

Barry Maitland

Following the murder of his young wife, Charles Verge, world famous architect and head of a very lucrative London practice, disappears without a trace. After four months of dead-end investigations, Chief Detective Inspector Brock and his team are called in to achieve the impossible: to find fresh leads and overlooked clues and to finally put an end to the much-discussed Verge mystery. Was this a crime of passion and has Verge escaped to Spain, or even Sydney, as the public sightings suggest? Or is Verge already dead, a victim of the murderer? From the suave world of international architecture to the backstreets of Barcelona, the only thing missing is Verge himself.

In their own often unorthodox style, Detective Chief Inspector David Brock and Detective Sergeant Kathy Kolla manage to unlock the secret that has perplexed and intrigued both the police investigation and the public imagination.

'Barry Maitland is a master of mysteries.' *Los Angeles Times Book Review*

'More, please, Mr Maitland.' *The Washington Times*

ISBN 1 74114 141 9